Christmas A

Christmas Angel Charity

Three Christmas Angels Series, Volume 3

Morris Fenris

Published by Changing Culture Publications (CCPUB), 2021.

CHRISTMAS ANGEL CHARITY

First edition. November 7, 2021.

Written by Morris Fenris.

Morris Fenris

Christmas Angel Charity

Three Christmas Angels Book Three

Copyright 2020 Morris Fenris, Changing Culture Publications

Prologue

Heaven's Guardian Angel School...

"**H**allelujah! Amen!"

The sound of the voices faded away as everyone paused, and Charity closed her eyes to savor the serenity of the moment. When she opened her eyes again, her fellow angels had similar looks upon their faces as they basked in this special moment.

"Very nice. Let's all take a bit of time to ourselves before the celebration starts. Polish your halos. Fluff your wings. Practice your smiles." The choirmaster smiled at them before leaving the room.

Charity followed her friends, Hope and Joy, out of the choir hall. She smiled at others they passed along the way. Her friends didn't seem to be as happy, but given the pressure being placed on all three of them in their current assignments, Charity completely understood.

"Let's go in here," Charity pointed to the schoolroom. The three friends needed to talk. They hoped to brainstorm some solutions for one another, including Charity's assignment.

Hope, Joy, and Charity were part of the guardian angel training school. All three were currently on probation for various infractions. Charity sat down and watched her friends do likewise. Hope dropped her head into her hands, but Joy looked so sad, it was hard to remember they'd just come from choir practice for the big Christmas celebration.

"Look at us," she murmured mostly to herself. "We sure aren't going to inspire anyone like this." The longer that Charity spent with her two morose friends, the less joy she was able to retain. Something had to be done if the three were going to fulfill their responsibilities to their human charges.

"What are you three angels doing? The celebration is about to begin," Matthias asked, startling all three.

In charge of training the newer guardian angels, Matthias had to approve of how they dealt with their charges. Charity tried to fake a smile for him but realized she had failed when he stopped at their table to tower over them. Charity dropped her eyes, not having any sort of answer to provide him. When none of them offered an answer to his question, he crossed his arms over his chest and made a noise letting them know his patience wasn't everlasting.

He cleared his throat to gain their attention and then met their eyes, one by one. "Well?"

"My little boy is so sad," Joy told him, tossing her hands out to her sides dramatically.

Matthias nodded in acknowledgement of her response and then looked to the next angel. "And you, Hope? The last time we talked you were excited about your current assignment."

"My charge doesn't even want to celebrate Christmas this year," Hope stated, huffing out a breath as she dropped her chin back into her cupped hands.

Charity listened while Hope talked about her charge, her mind going to her own charge and the problems she presented.

"But the idea behind Christmas has nothing to do with those things," Matthias reminded Hope, bringing Charity back to the present.

"I know that," Hope nodded, "but in my charges file, she loved all of those things, until a year ago. Now, she abhors the very idea of Christmas. I'm trying not to hold that against her, but it's very hard, I must confess. Christmas is the most wonderful time of the year, but my charge hates it."

"Well, at least your charge doesn't visit the cemetery every day. It's really sad to watch her cry, day after day, and not even try to get on with living her life," Charity added, deciding it was better to offer information before Matthias asked for it. She was the most mature of the angels in training and had already successfully completed two of the required three special assignments. If successful in helping her current charge overcome a soul-searing grief, she would graduate at the end of January.

Hope and Joy still had to successfully help their first charge before they could even think about helping their second. While Charity sympathized with her friends' plights, she had her own struggle to deal with. She had a charge who was completely overwhelmed with a grief that Charity hadn't even been able to discover. It was time to ask Matthias for help going through the archives. Charity was pretty sure she was missing some piece of the puzzle that would help her ease the sorrow of her current charge.

Matthias looked at the three and then shook his head, "So you three are just going to sit around up here, moaning about your difficult situations rather than try to find a solution to them?"

Joy looked up at him, "What are we supposed to do? I mean, it's only a few weeks before Christmas. How are people supposed to remember they're celebrating the birth of the Christ Child if they are so unhappy?"

Matthias grinned, "You find a way to make them happy. Help them remember the good things in life and give them hope. Hope is what Christmas is all about. Your job is to try and get your charges to see that. That's your job. Remember, a guardian angel doesn't just keep their charge from getting run over as they cross the street, you also have to help your charge in the emotional, spiritual, and mental realm."

The three angels looked at each other and their expressions slowly started to change. Hope was the first to speak up as a new idea began to form.

"I could help Claire want to celebrate Christmas."

"And I could help Maddie find another outlet for her grief," added Charity. "What about you, Joy? Why is your little boy so sad?"

"My little boy wants his mama to not be so sad. She's lonely and he wants to help her but doesn't know how."

"Maybe she needs a puppy to love?" Hope suggested with a smile.

"Puppies are nice. So are kittens," Charity offered. "This time of year, there are always an abundance of both at the animal shelters. Maybe your little charge's mother could adopt a new pet?"

Matthias squatted down so that he was eye-level with the littlest of the three angels. "You'll find a way. I have faith in you."

"Thanks?" Joy queried, wishing she had as much faith in herself as the head of the angel school seemed to have. "Maybe we should brainstorm some more ideas..."

Matthias shook his head, "That is not going to happen while I'm around. I'm still recovering from the last brainstorming session you three had together. If you need to bounce ideas off of someone, I am always available to you."

Hope exchanged glances with Joy and Charity, both of them feeling embarrassed over being reminded of their previous failures.

Joy was the first to speak up, "I guess I should probably get back down there, huh?"

"That would be a good place to start," Matthias agreed with a nod and warm smile. "You should all be busy trying to help your charges right now. Christmas is only two weeks away and you all should know better than anyone just how fast time can fly. Go and tend to your charges and remember, I am always here if you need advice or just to talk through a plan."

Hope, Charity and Joy nodded dutifully, "Thank you."

Matthias smiled at each of them. "Off with you all now. Go enjoy the celebration for a bit and then take that enthusiasm back to your duties. We'll have even more to celebrate once you three have your charges sorted out."

Charity nodded, a course of action starting to form in her head. Maddie Jacobs had grieved long enough, if only Charity knew what that was, it would make her job so much easier. That was where Matthias was going to have to help her. Maddie seemed to be stuck and unless Charity could figure out what had put her in that position, she wouldn't have much chance of getting her to move forward with her life.

Joy smiled, "I'm heading down there right now. Thanks, Matthias."

"What about the celebration?" Hope asked her. Charity followed Hope's gaze, watching the other angels beginning to gather around the center courtyard. The choir performance was about to start. "We're going to sing soon."

Joy shook her head, smiling brightly as she replied, "There's so much to be thankful for and happy about this time of year. I don't need a celebration to remind me of that. I just need to figure out how to make Sam's dream come true and then everything will work out just fine."

Matthias smiled approvingly at her. "Good luck to you, Joy. I look forward to hearing a good report from you. Charity and Hope, good luck to you as well. The miracles of Christmas are just beginning."

Hope and Charity nodded and then headed across the yard to where the chorus was taking their places. Charity smiled at the other angels who were quickly finding their places and preparing themselves for the celebration. It was Christmas in Heaven and on Earth. Even though there were still a few weeks before the humans would actually celebrate in remembrance of the birth of the Christ Child, they'd been celebrating for several weeks in Heaven. Each day it grew closer to December 25th, the celebrations grew bigger and more meaningful.

This was Charity's favorite time of year, especially since she got to spend a large portion of it on Earth. This year, her charge lived in the State of Montana. She loved snow, and Montana had a bunch of it this year. Hope tapped her on the shoulder, and Charity realized she'd allowed her mind to drift briefly.

She nodded her thanks and then turned her attention to the center of the courtyard and watched as the choirmaster took his place at the podium.

"Alright, is everyone ready?" the choirmaster smiled. When everyone nodded, he lifted his hands, and brought them down as the sound of angelic praises filled the heavenly skies.

"Gloria. In excelsis deo. Gloria. In excelsis deo."

Charity sang out and half an hour later she felt renewed once again and capable of tackling the problem her charge was having. Regardless of what it was. She parted ways with Hope, but instead of heading back down to check on Maddie, she went in search of Matthias.

She found him sitting on the steps of the library, as if he was waiting for someone. She slowly approached him, surprised when he smiled at her arrival and then stood up and walked beside her. "Let's go see if we can solve your problem, little angel."

Charity gave him a curious look and then asked, "You were waiting for me?"

"Of course. I could tell you were puzzled about something, and I sensed you would come look for me. So, what is happening with your charge?"

"That's what I would like to know," Charity informed him. "She visits the cemetery every day, without fail. She spends half an hour, sometimes a bit longer, and then leaves—often, in tears—and goes to work only to return a few hours later. I overheard the gardener at the cemetery talking to a co-worker, and they are puzzled as well. She's been doing this same thing for over a year since whoever's gravesite she visits was placed there."

"Where does she work?" Matthias asked as he opened up the door to the archival room.

"She's a nurse but she doesn't seem to be taking any joy in helping others. Her co-workers are very worried about her as well."

Charity followed him inside and then waited while he located Maddie's file. "So, what exactly do you want to know? I'm limited in how much information I can share with you at this time."

Charity gave him a quizzical look, "Why is that?"

"This is your third challenge and part of your duties include discovering how best to help your charge. If I simply handed you everything you needed to know, you wouldn't get to know your charge nearly as well."

Charity nodded, understanding that thinking, but not liking it any better. "If it makes you feel any better about helping me now, I've been following Maddie for weeks now but once she leaves the cemetery, she goes to her job and then she returns to the cemetery. When it gets too late or she gets too cold, she returns home, eats barely enough to keep a mouse alive, and then falls into bed. She gets up the next day and repeats it all over again. She doesn't seem to have many friends, at least, not ones that she interacts with much. She goes to church every Sunday morning, but she arrives shortly after the service has started, always going by the cemetery first, and always sits on the back pew. She leaves the minute the preacher says, 'Amen' and doesn't hang around to talk to anyone."

"What about family?" Matthias asked.

"She talks to her mother on the phone once a week and always paints a picture of happiness and sunshine for herself. The only other phone call she gets comes in once a week, but Maddie merely watches the phone's screen until the call goes to voicemail and then she takes a bath and cries for a while."

Matthias frowned and then started up the archival replay program. "Let's go back a year and see what is missing."

Charity watched as Maddie appeared on the screen, with a smile on her face and looking completely different. She was in a bridal shop, trying on a wedding gown, and a woman Charity didn't recognize was nodding and smiling at her.

"I don't recognize that happy woman. She's so different from the woman I see now."

"Let's move forward a few weeks."

Charity nodded and when the screen lit back up, she saw Maddie, dressed all in black, at the cemetery, sobbing brokenly as a casket was lowered into the ground. Her grief was all-consuming, and several people came over and tried to offer her comfort, but she ignored them all. The woman who had been in the bridal shop with her approached, tears streaming down her face, a folded United States flag held in her hands.

After a brief conversation, the older woman handed Maddie the flag and then walked away, grief in every step she took. Maddie clasped the flag to her chest and then sank to the snowy ground, fresh tears streaming down her face.

Charity felt tears stinging her own eyes as she was filled with compassion for the young woman on the screen. She surreptitiously wiped them away and then asked quietly, "Who died?"

Matthias cleared his throat, clearly also overcome with emotion over the young woman's past. "Jeremiah Shaw. They were to have been married right after the New Year when he came home from his second tour of duty in the Middle East."

Charity gasped as understanding dawned. "He was killed in action."

"Yes. He and five of his squad were on patrol when their Humvee hit an IED. No one survived."

"How horrible. No wonder she visits the grave every day. She was planning to spend the rest of her life with Jeremiah," Charity murmured. *And in some way is continuing to do so.*

Matthias turned off the screen and then looked at her, "You have your work cut out for you."

"I can see that. Now that I know what sorrow she's dealing with, maybe I can find a way to help her remember the past and look forward to the future."

"Good luck. If you need anything else, don't hesitate to ask. This is your third assignment and I look forward to watching you graduate."

"I'm looking forward to that day as well. Thank you again for your assistance."

Charity left Matthias and headed for Montana and her charge. Maddie was only twenty-three years old and yet it seemed as if she believed her life was now over. Charity meant to correct that, and she only had a few weeks to do so. Christmas was right around the corner and Charity needed to have her charge's problem fixed before then. She definitely had her work cut out for her.

Chapter 1

December 12ᵗʰ,
Great Falls, Montana...

"Here she comes again," said Joe Walsh, the head gardener at Memorial Gardens cemetery.

"It's freezing out there this morning," Stan, the assistant gardener murmured. He joined his boss at the window in the gardener's building and watched the small, red Civic park and a young woman get out and head for a headstone that was twenty yards away.

"I cleared the snow away from the gravesite," Joe commented. "I wish someone could do something for her. I've seen people grieve before, but never like this."

"It's not healthy," Stan agreed. "Maybe I'll wander that direction and see if she'll talk to me today."

Joe shrugged, "I tried that last night when she showed up here just before sunset. It was only twenty degrees outside, and she still visited that grave."

"She's dedicated, that's for sure." Stan pulled his hat and gloves on and zipped up his winter parka before stepping out of the warm building and getting into the small golf cart they used to get around the cemetery. He headed for the lone figure, currently crouched low in front of the headstone with her head bowed. As he drew nearer, he could see her shoulders shaking slightly and realized she was crying again.

He stopped the cart and approached her quietly. The crunch of his feet moving through the new fallen snow was the only sound.

"Miss?"

She lifted tear-stained eyes to him and then whispered, "Yes?"

"Miss, it's very cold today. You come here twice a day, every day, but with the weather as it is, we're very concerned for your health."

"I'm fine. I don't even feel the cold," she assured him back.

"That may be, but there's a winter storm watch in effect from noon on until the end of the week. We've been instructed to close the gates and..."

"No! Oh, please. You can't close the cemetery," she pleaded with him, getting to her feet and wrapping her arms around her torso. She looked back at the gate, as if gauging the distance she would need to walk if they closed the gates as they'd been instructed.

"Miss, I'm sure whomever you're visiting here will understand if you can't visit for a few days. It's your health we're concerned about."

"I...," she looked at him and Stan almost buckled in his resolve to follow orders. Then she seemed to deflate and nodded a few times. "I understand. I'll leave... If I could just have a few more minutes?"

"Of course," Stan offered, retreating back to the cart. He headed back to the building and then watched, along with Joe, until she finally got up and headed back to her vehicle. "I feel horrible for doing that to her."

"It's for her own good. Besides, do you want to come out here and fight the feet of snow we're supposed to get overnight?"

"Not particularly," Stan agreed. "Maybe this little break will be good for her. How long's it been since we put that casket in the ground?"

"Twelve months and a few weeks."

"Definitely time for her to take a break."

. . ⚓ . .

MADDIE GOT BACK INTO her car and turned the heat on full blast. Her fingers needed a few minutes to thaw out. She'd been running late this morning and had forgotten to grab her gloves off the rack in front of the fireplace. She was beginning a new position at the hospital this morning but visiting Miah's gravesite had taken precedence over going back for something as silly as her gloves.

She examined the skin, frowning when she saw how red her fingertips were. "I need another pair of gloves to leave in the car, so this doesn't happen again." She buckled her seatbelt and then put the car in gear before navigating the winding road of the cemetery until she reached the stone gate. She paused there. The gardener's words about the snowstorm and the cemetery being closed for the remainder of the week came back to her.

She glanced at the clock on her dashboard and realized, if she didn't leave now, she was going to be late. Knowing she wouldn't be able to visit Miah for several days was a physical pain in her chest. Fresh tears filled her eyes, and she took a calming breath before forcing herself to release the brake and pull out onto the road.

She had herself together once more when she reached the hospital, and she quickly changed into her scrubs and headed up to the pediatric floor. A year ago, being assigned to the pediatric ward was all she'd wanted, but there hadn't been any openings. Now, she'd been given one of the most prized nursing positions, and she was struggling to find any excitement for the job. She'd actually given thought to declining the promotion, but that would have prompted an inquiry into her life that she'd gone to great lengths the last few months to keep hidden. Everyone thought she was doing fine and getting on with her life. If they knew...well, she'd probably find herself having to talk to a grief counselor. She wasn't sure she could handle that kind of probing.

"Maddie, aren't you so excited to be working up on the third floor now?" Jamie, one of her co-workers gushed as she joined her in the elevator.

"I've always wanted to work up there," Maddie gave a pat response.

"Well, looks like your dreams are coming true." Jamie winked at her. The elevator stopped on the second floor, and she got off. "Have fun. I hear Christmas time up there is a ball."

Maddie forced a smile and nodded. "I'll do my best." She was relieved once the elevator doors closed, and she was alone once more. It didn't last long. Soon, the doors opened, and she stepped into what appeared to be an attempt to turn the pediatric ward into Santa's workshop. Christmas music rang out over the speakers, streamers, balloons, Christmas trees, and fake snow were everywhere she looked.

She slowly walked toward the nurses' station in the center of the floor, avoiding children who were navigating the halls on crutches and in wheelchairs, all decorated in line with the holiday season. She came to a stop when she reached the nurses' station and observed the four ladies she would be working with on a continual basis. Instead of the maroon hospital issued scrubs Maddie was currently wearing, the nurses were all dressed in scrubs depicting various images of Christmas, and elf hats. Elf hats with fake pointy ears attached, no less.

"Hi! You must be Maddie," one of the older nurses noticed her.

Maddie nodded, "I'm kind of wondering if I'm in the right place."

"You're most definitely in the right place. Go on back to the employee lounge and you'll find a selection of scrubs in your size. We do everything we can to make this place *not* look like a hospital, especially this time of year."

Maddie nodded and then carefully made her way to the employee lounge. She found a locker with her name attached in glitter paint, and inside were four sets of scrubs. Green scrubs that had Christmas lights running up and down and all around them, Red scrubs with snowmen and reindeer dancing across the fabric, blue scrubs with more snowmen and snowflakes, and then a soft pink pair of scrubs with scene from "The Nutcracker" depicted on them.

She sighed and blindly reached for scrubs, ending up with the green scrubs. She changed, and then made her way back to the nurses' station, feeling silly and not at all in the holiday spirit. She waited for someone to notice her, cringing when someone did and immediately noticed she wasn't wearing her elf ears.

"Hey, you forgot your hat. Here, we always have a few extra lying around. Some of the doctors like to join in on our fun when they come up to do rounds."

Maddie took the hat and gingerly put it on, hoping it wasn't going to get in the way of her performing her duties. "Okay, so point me in the right direction, and I'll get started."

"First, let's introduce you to everyone. "This is Shelia, the only CNA we have today because Marci has the stomach flu and is staying home for a few days."

"Sounds like a good plan," Maddie concurred.

"I'm Penny, that's Ciera, and this is Teresa. There's another crew of us that comes in for the night shift, but you won't ever see them since your shift ends at 4:30."

"Nice to meet you all. I'm Maddie."

"We're glad to have you up here. We've been short a nurse for the last three months, and I was beginning to think we weren't ever going to get a new team member. Come with me and I'll introduce you to some of our long-term residents." Teresa grabbed a pile of charts and headed down the hallway with Maddie tagging along.

"Long-term?"

"Yeah, most of them have been here for weeks or even months. The majority of them are here because this was a better option for their chemo treatments than traveling somewhere else, and we are beginning to get a pretty good reputation for our work with kids dealing with cancer. We also have one kiddo in renal failure. She gets dialysis every other day while she's waiting for a donor match."

Maddie nodded. "And the rest of the patients?"

"The usual childhood things. Appendix or tonsil removals. Broken arms or legs. Concussions. We don't keep the infectious disease patients up here on the floor any longer since they pose a significant threat to the cancer kiddos, but everything else pediatric related comes to us."

"Okay. So, how do you divide up the floor?"

Teresa smiled and shook her head. "We don't. Because we never know what emergency is going to pop up. We're also dealing with little kids who might or might not have someone they trust nearby when things fall apart, so we make sure we all touch base with every patient, every shift. We want to build their trust in all of us so that we can better treat them in a crisis situation."

"That actually makes a lot of sense," Maddie murmured, thinking of the chaos such a system would create on any other floor. With shift nurses and a constant influx of new patients and new staff, getting to know your patient almost never happened.

Maddie followed Teresa around the rest of the morning, getting to know the patients and their parents, and also getting used to the unorthodox way this floor was run. It worked, and that was the most surprising thing of all.

"Maddie, you've only got thirty minutes until your shift ends. You need to make sure and document everything at the end of each shift so you can get started on that now."

Maddie glanced at the clock, shocked to see that the day was indeed almost over for her. "Thanks, I didn't realize how quickly the day had gone."

"Things move fast around here," Sheila

"I'm seeing that." She sat down at the computer and began documenting her interaction with the patients. The rest of her day had been more than a little bit unorthodox, but documenting patient files was familiar and she took comfort in the tedious task.

Chapter 2

D r. Nick Stavros looked at the images on the computer screen in front of him, feeling a sense of relief so strong that he had to fight back tears. He'd spent the day performing surgeries and helping some of his youngest cancer patients get through the various treatments designed to give them a chance at beating the diseased cells trying to kill them. It was the least favorite part of his job, but necessary. He made it a point to try and instill hope in each and every one of his patients.

He glanced at the lab results one more time, a small sense of relief dispelling some of the shadows in his soul. The news was good and meant that at least one of his patients would live to finish high school and become an adult. It was these moments that gave him the strength to keep coming to work each day. It was also these moments he clung to when the lab results weren't good and the report he had to give his patient and their family was the worst. Thankfully, he only had good news to deliver today.

"Doctor, they just took the last patient back upstairs. Is it okay for us to start cleaning up the suite?" one of his nurses asked.

Nick nodded and smiled at her. "Of course. Today's been a long and trying day. Send everyone home early once things are set to rights. Thankfully, we don't have anyone scheduled for chemo or radiation tomorrow so we can all catch up on paperwork and the like."

"Yes, doctor." The nurse turned to leave and then hesitated. She turned around and Nick raised a brow at the question he could see in her eyes.

"Yes? Was there something else you needed?"

"Just...well, the girls and I were talking, and...what's to become of Zachary? I glanced at his scans. With today's treatment, he might just beat this thing."

Nick tapped the computer monitor in front of him and nodded. "He's definitely going to beat this thing. As far as what's in his future, I'm working on it." Nick didn't give away any indication of how he was working on it, just that the nurses didn't need to worry because he was at the helm and handling things.

"Well, I know I speak for everyone else...if you need any help just ask."

"Thank you. I'll definitely keep that in mind."

"Good. Well, goodnight," the nurse smiled at him and then left the doctor's lounge.

Once again, he was alone with his thoughts and the images on the screen before him. He took a few measurements and then typed a quick note to the radiologist who would perform a more thorough reading later that night. Once that was finished, he typed a few notes in the computer, documenting his observations about the treatments his patients had received today, and then he logged out and closed the screens.

A glance at the clock showed it was only 3:30 and not quite time for him to go upstairs and see his patients one last time before heading home for the evening. His stomach reminded him that he hadn't stopped for lunch. He turned the lights off as he headed for the first-floor cafeteria. As far as hospital food went, the hospital here was second to none. Cook to order grills, and a meal of the day were always available, twenty-four-seven. They also had a nice selection of deli-type fare; pastries from a local bakery and every kind of juice and soft drink imaginable.

Nick grabbed a turkey sandwich, a large cup of coffee, and topped his meal off with a cookie. He let the attendant scan everything and then supplied his I.D. card and had the amount charged to his personal account. He didn't converse with her as she seemed intent on continuing her conversation with the other attendant. Nick thought it was slightly rude, but he wasn't the head of Human Resources, and he didn't need any self-made aggravation today.

"Dr. Stavros," a voice called as he entered the dining area.

Nick looked to his right and then nodded at Dr. Julia Stansfield. She was currently the head of Microbiology and spent much of her time in the laboratory bent over one petri dish or another. Nick and she had met when he'd first come to Montana. She had made it very clear that she was single and found him very eligible.

Nick had tried to be friendly and let her know that he wasn't interested in dating just yet, but she continued to seek him out. In this situation, if he ignored her offer to let him sit with her, it would appear very rude. He changed direction, but instead of sitting right next to her like she intended, he sat at the side of the table, far enough away that she couldn't accidentally touch him unless she was deliberately trying.

"Julia, how's your day going?"

"Just fine. How about you? You look so tired," she murmured, giving him a soft look.

"My day's actually been great. We received several reports of kids that are almost in remission. A few more treatments for some and then hopefully they'll be cancer free and remain so."

"That's wonderful news! Congratulations." She did reach across the table then and touch his hand.

Nick immediately moved it, pretending he was just picking up his sandwich. "I think so," he replied, taking a bite of his sandwich so he didn't have to say anything else.

"We should go out and celebrate. I hear the new Asian Fusion place downtown is amazing," she hinted.

Nick frowned and shook his head, taking a drink before commenting. "I'm afraid I'm not much of one for Asian food, in any fashion. I'm not a great lover of fish, and definitely not of anything raw. I would think you'd have similar concerns, dealing with microbes all day long."

"Well, I don't eat just any sushi, but I hear the food at the Coconut Fan is awesome. Are you sure you won't join me?"

Nick shook his head, "I really can't. I still have rounds to do and then several hours of charts to get through before morning."

"That's too bad. I was really hoping we could spend some time together."

Nick nodded and then decided he needed to restate his position where she was concerned. "I get that, but I thought we already discussed this. I'm not dating right now and maybe not in the near future. I have lots of things coming up that require my undivided attention."

"All work and no play…"

"Makes Dr. Stavros good at his job," Nick interjected before she could finish her statement. He finished his sandwich and then wadded up the paper. He finished his coffee and stood up, tucking the uneaten cookie into his pocket.

"I should probably get back to work. It was nice seeing you again," he told her with a smile.

She attempted to smile back at him, but it never reached her eyes. He headed for the elevator, pushing thoughts of Julia aside and getting into the mindset of caring for his patients once more. She was a complication he didn't need in his life. Ever.

He got off the elevator and smiled as he watched a group of children trying to decorate human trees with crepe paper. There seemed to be two teams of kids, each one of them consisting of kids who could walk on their own, and kids in wheelchairs or on crutches. He leaned against the doorway and watched as helpers encouraged the kids to work faster and together.

One team finally ran out of green crepe paper and was declared the winner to the shouts of delight from everyone. Even the losing team. Nick smiled, reminding himself that this ward was partly his dream come to life. Getting a diagnosis of cancer was such devastating news, and studies had proven that a proper mindset could make all of the difference in whether a child recovered or not. Nick had set out to make sure this pediatric ward was full of fun, laughter, and silliness; the trifecta needed for children to fight for their lives.

Nick stepped forward, clapping his hands and giving hi-fives to the children as he walked amongst them. "Great job, guys. I don't know if I've ever seen such lovely Christmas trees here in the hospital."

"Dr. Nick come sing with us," Melanie urged him. She grabbed his hand and started pulling him over toward the piano in the corner.

"One song, and then I need to go check on some of your friends and see if they're feeling any better. A couple of them had a rough day," he quietly informed Melanie and a few of the older children.

"We'll cheer them up later," they all promised, and Nick smiled and nodded. Laughter was often the best medicine and at times could help those who were hurting focus on something besides the pain while the medicine kicked in and did its job.

"I know you will. So, what are we singing?"

He sat down at the piano and grinned when they all started chanting, "Rudolph! Rudolph!"

"Rudolph it is," he winked at them. He ran his hands over the keys and, after doing a little impromptu introduction, he launched into the song. His deep baritone voice filled the small room alongside with the children's voices and a few adult ones from parents who couldn't help but join in.

"You know...Dasher, and Dancer, and Prancer, and Vixen. Comet, and Cupid, and Donner, and Blitzen. But do you recall?" he paused and the children who had participated on the song before answered, "No!"

"The most famous reindeer of all," he did an elaborate walk down the piano keys and ended up on a deep roll. He looked at Melanie and asked, "You going to help me out?"

She nodded, and he smiled and began, "Rudolph the red-nosed reindeer."

"Reindeer," Melanie supplied amidst giggles from the others.

"Had a very shiny nose."

"Like a lightbulb," one of the other children sang out.

"And if you ever saw it."

"Saw it," Melanie's soft voice echoed him.

"You would even say it glows."

"Like a flashlight," the children all joined in.

"All of the other reindeer."

"Reindeer," everyone was joining in the fun now.

"Used to laugh and call him names."

"Like Pinocchio."

"They never let poor Rudolph."

"Rudolph."

"Join in any reindeer games."

"Like Monopoly." More giggles erupted at the silliness.

"Then one foggy Christmas Eve, Santa came to say."

"Ho, Ho, Ho."

Nick paused and then whispered loudly, "Everyone now."

"Rudolph, with your nose so bright, won't you guide my sleigh tonight."

Nick grinned at the kids as they let their voices get dramatic.

"Then all the reindeer loved him."

"Loved him."

"As they shouted out with glee."

"Yippee!"

"Rudolph the red-nosed reindeer."

"Reindeer."

"You'll go down in history."

"Like George Washington."

Nick made a big production of the last phrase, ending with a grand finale on the piano. "That was awesome, guys." He'd taken piano lessons for years while he was younger and had always tried to incorporate the power of music into his practice of medicine. Adding a piano to the common room on the third floor of the hospital had been one of his first requisitions. Based on the sea of smiling faces surrounding him, it was one of his better ideas.

"Can you sing another one with us?" Melanie pleaded.

"Maybe after I finish checking on your friends." He tousled the small fuzz on Melanie's head and grinned back at her. "You guys continue whatever games you were playing, and I'll stop back by here and see you all in a bit."

He shook hands with a few lingering parents and then made his way toward the center of the floor and the nurses' station. He rounded the corner and then stopped when he spied a new head behind the desk. Well, to be correct, the head was new and wearing elf ears and a corny hat, but still...she was still new.

She was sitting in front of the computer screen and had her head down when he approached. He took a moment to observe her, liking the way her blonde hair shone, what he could see of it at least. She was wearing the green scrubs and he smiled, wondering what her take had been on the way this floor was run.

Dr. Nick Stavros could have gone anywhere in the country, but he'd chosen to come here with a few conditions. First, the children's floor was his domain. He dictated how it was run down to the scrubs which the nurses wore. He believed that healing children wasn't just a matter of medicine but also of environment. It was the hospital's duty to provide the best healing atmosphere possible. In return for him agreeing to stay here and add prestige to their facility, he got to say where, when, and how high. At least on this floor.

The new head behind the desk still hadn't seen him, so he stepped forward, watching as his shadow fell across her screen and anxious to see what color her eyes were. Pretty nurses didn't normally do anything for Nick, but already there was something about this one that told him things were going to be different with her. He'd been given files on four nurses from other areas in the hospital, all of which had expressed a desire to work in pediatrics at some point in their career at the hospital. Nick had drug his feet for weeks before finally opening up the files and choosing a candidate. This was the newest member to the nursing staff, and he hoped the photo that had been included in her file hadn't just been a fluke.

Her picture had shown a young woman with compassionate eyes, a lovely smile, and he'd immediately known there was something special about her. When he'd talked to her supervisor, he'd gotten nothing but a good report, although the director of nursing had suggested that a change of scenery would be ideal for the young nurse right now. Nick had asked for an explanation, but the director of nursing had simply told him she'd suffered a great personal loss a year ago and seemed to have gotten stuck in a rut.

Nick hadn't even thought twice about telling HR to offer her the position. That had been three weeks ago and, while he remembered the impression her picture had left, he couldn't for the life of him remember what color her eyes were.

He didn't know why she'd left such an impression upon him. He'd take time to consider that later. Right now, he just needed to know. Were her eyes blue, green, or some other color combination?

Okay, look up.

Chapter 3

M addie was almost finished with her patient reports when a shadow fell over her. She looked up into the bluest eyes she'd ever seen. They were watching her carefully, and she suddenly felt very self-conscious with the elf hat on her head.

"You're new here," a very deep and soothing voice told her. She dropped her eyes to his mouth and then let them travel up to take in the rest of his face.

"I just started today."

"Well, then. Welcome to Jollyville."

"Jollyville?" Maddie questioned.

The man stood up and she guessed he must be at least 6'2", if not just an inch taller. "Dr. Stavros, at your service. And you are?"

"Maddie Jacobs."

"Nice to meet you, Miss Maddie. Are you just finishing up your shift?"

Maddie glanced at the clock and then nodded, "I have fifteen minutes left."

"Perfect. Come with me," he said, smiling. Maddie found herself following him to a room at the end of the hallway. She'd yet to meet the occupant of the long-term room as they had been receiving some extensive treatment and had only been brought back up to the floor an hour earlier.

Maddie held back as Dr. Stavros gloved up, and then she followed suit. "Zachary had some pretty awful chemo and radiation earlier today. I kept him down in recovery where I could check on him frequently until the worst of the nausea was gone. Hopefully, this is the last such treatment Zachary will need to tolerate, but it was one of the most intensive. His little body has been through so much these last few months...I just hope and pray I don't have to put him through any more."

Maddie nodded and then quietly followed the doctor into the darkened room. Dr. Stavros approached the bed and flipped on the nightlights that shone directly onto the ceiling, illuminating the room with a dim glow instead of a bright light.

"Hey, little man. How's my champ doing now?"

"Better, Nick. I don't feel like puking much now. I just hurt."

"Where are you hurting, bud, and we'll see what we can do to get rid of it," asked Dr. Stavros, whom she'd just learned was named Nick.

"I don't suppose you'd believe everywhere?"

"After what you went through today, I would. I brought a new friend with me. This is Maddie."

"Hi, Maddie. I like your elf ears," Zachary told her softly.

"Thank you," she smiled down at him, hiding the emotions his physically frail body conjured up inside of her. He was completely bald, and there were dark shadows beneath his eyes. His arms were frail, and his skin had a grey pallor to it. This little boy had been to hell and back, and it broke her heart.

"Maybe Maddie can go and get us some pain medication for you, huh?" Nick asked. When Zach gave a weak nod, he murmured what he required, and Maddie quickly left the room and headed for the pharmacy room. She retrieved the vials of medication, logged them out and then hurried back to Zach's room. She watched as Nick expertly administered the medication and then sat by Zach's side while the medication took effect and the young man drifted off to sleep.

When it seemed that Zach was going to rest peacefully for a while, Nick stood and motioned for Maddie to join him. In the hallway, he took a moment and tipped his head back, squeezing the bridge of his nose between two fingers and taking several deep and measured breaths. When he looked down, he gave her an apologetic smile.

"Sorry, some kids get to you more than others. Zach is the bravest kid I know and, after today, he has a real chance of beating this thing."

"His parents must be very excited about that news," she told him.

Nick shook his head and then clenched his fist. "I'm sure they would be if they were around to hear the news. Zach's mom was killed in a car crash when he was six months old. His dad was in the Marines, stationed in Afghanistan when Zach got sick. His dad and I were best buddies growing up back in Louisiana. When Jeff heard Zach had been diagnosed with cancer, he asked me to go and get him. I brought him back here along with his grandmother, but she couldn't handle watching Zach get so sick. She went back home two months ago."

"She just left her grandson here?" Maddie asked, outraged on Zach's behalf.

"She'd been here for almost five months and her health wasn't all that good. Her daughter insisted she come home and bring Zach with her, but I refused to sign off on his medical transfer."

"Surely she could understand that he was too fragile to move?" Maddie stated.

"He wasn't, I just didn't want to let him go. Jeff was killed in action a few weeks after I brought Zachary out here to Montana."

Maddie felt her heart clench at the mention of being killed in action. She did her best to hide her reaction as Nick continued to talk.

Zachary's like me. He lost someone he never should have.

"Jeff's parents had him late in life and were already gone, and he was an only child. Sarah's mother Clara, the grandmother who was taking care of Zach, hates the snow and just wanted to be back home in a place that's she familiar with. She has the beginning stages of Alzheimer disease, and I fully concurred with her returning to her home."

"So, Zach has no one?" Maddie couldn't help asking the question, giving voice to the thoughts in her head. *Zachary is exactly like me. All alone.* Only Maddie wasn't truly alone, she'd just chosen to live that way.

Nick gave her a sharp look, "He has me. And once he gets well enough to be discharged, I'm going to petition the courts for guardianship of him. Right now, I only have medical power of attorney, but that will end once he's well enough to be discharged."

"Are the courts likely to rule in your favor?" Maddie asked, noticing that they'd returned to the nurses' station. Her conversation with the gorgeous doctor hadn't gone unnoticed.

"They will. They have to," he told her with a small grin. "Teresa, how is Paula doing?"

"Much better. That drain appears to be working well and hasn't clogged once all day."

"Good. Maddie, it was good to meet you." Nick nodded at everyone else, grabbed a handful of candy canes from the bright red bucket sitting on the counter and then proceeded to whistle his way down the hallway.

"Girl, you move fast. Good job!" Sheila told her with a big grin.

"What?" Maddie asked, feeling as if she'd just fallen into a rabbit hole.

"Nick Stavros is the hottest doctor on staff and incredibly single. He doesn't flirt with any of the other nurses..."

"Until now," Teresa replied. "He seems to only run away from nurses and the like that can't take a hint."

Sheila looked at her and winked, "She's referring to that doctor down in the lab. She's had her sights set on becoming Mrs. Nick Stavros since he first came here."

"He wasn't flirting with me. He was telling me about Zach..."

"Ah, Zach is his special patient. Nick doesn't take just anyone down to meet him. You've definitely caught his eye."

Maddie shook her head and felt the elf ears tip sideways. She pulled the hat off and laid it on the counter. "I don't want to catch anyone's eyes. I'll see you ladies tomorrow."

She hurriedly changed and then rushed to her vehicle. It was already dark, but she drove the familiar path to the cemetery, ignoring the way her car slid on the ice and how fast the snow was coming down. It wasn't until she reached the gates and saw them shut and locked that she remembered what the gardener had told her earlier that morning.

The cemetery's going to be closed for the rest of the week.

She felt like crying and considered walking across the lawn to reach Miah's grave, but she didn't have her boots on and had forgotten her gloves. She'd be risking her own health and for what, a few minutes alone with him while the wind howled?

A little voice inside her head reminded here that Miah wasn't actually in that grave, just the remains of his body were interned there. Miah had been a believer and that meant he was in Heaven, but Maddie had a hard time letting her mind go there. She and Miah had planned their entire future out and without him here, she'd been drifting on a sea of sorrow that never seemed to end. The ritual of visiting Miah both morning and night had kept her sane and now...well, what was she supposed to do now?

She sat in the car, and she closed her eyes for a moment. "God, I don't know why this is happening. All I wanted to do was talk to him, tell him about my day...isn't it enough that you took him from me in physical form, and now you're trying to prevent me from even being able to visit him while he's in the ground? You should have just taken me as well. I died that day he got blown up, just as much as he did."

Depressed and finding it difficult to make herself drive home, she finally turned the car around and inched her way back to her small apartment. This had been a very long day. With her usual routine disrupted, she entered her apartment and was at odds for what to do with the remaining hours before bedtime. She didn't normally spend lots of time at the grave after working a full shift, but having her schedule disrupted had sent her into a mental tailspin. She couldn't quite figure out how to fill those extra minutes.

She sat on the couch and stared at the television which she hadn't turned it on in over a year. She briefly glanced around, wondering where she'd last seen the remote. After ten minutes, she finally located it on a bookshelf and retrieved it. The local news was talking about the winter storm. She stared at the screen, letting the voices and sounds wash over her as she dealt with being unable to share her day with Miah for the first time in over a year.

It felt odd and unnatural. She finally gave up and laid down on the couch, succumbing to sleep and a brief respite from the exhaustion and sadness that seemed to be her constant companions. The ringing of the phone woke her up several hours later, and she groggily looked at the clock on her phone, feeling a sense of despair settle in the pit of her stomach.

She swung her legs around on the couch and stared at the phone hanging on the wall, mentally counting the rings. *Two. Three. Four.*

The phone went silent. The answering machine picked up as tears of frustration filled her eyes.

Maddie, it's Brenda. I don't know if you ever listen to my messages, or if maybe you're listening to me now and just can't make yourself pick up the phone...I won't quit trying to talk to you. I love you just as much as I loved Jeremiah and I keep hoping you'll let me back into your life. Please...if you won't talk to me or your mom, find someone to talk to. I know you're still hurting; we all are, but Jeremiah wouldn't want things to be this way between us.

I wanted you to know that I'm thinking about coming to Great Falls for Christmas and I was hoping maybe you would agree to meet me for coffee or maybe even lunch? I miss you, Maddie. You're the daughter I never had, and I really would like to see you.

Please, consider calling me back. I love you, dear. I'm praying for you every day. Well...have a good rest of your evening.

Maddie pressed a fist against her mouth to keep from crying out loud. Brenda had been like a second mom to her. She'd tried to help Maddie deal with things right after the funeral, but Maddie had pushed her and everyone else away. When Brenda's sister had invited her to move to Colorado a few weeks after the funeral, so that she wouldn't be alone, Brenda had reluctantly agreed to go. Moving hadn't stopped her weekly calls, however. Brenda called at precisely eight o'clock every Thursday evening, and Maddie sat or stood in her apartment and listened to her messages, never once picking up the phone in the past ten years.

She didn't hate Brenda, but Maddie didn't talk about Miah or his passing. With anyone. In her mind, that would make it all the more real and she needed to keep herself together. She was operating under the assumption that if she faked it long enough, eventually she'd get to the point where she wouldn't have to. Also, if she didn't talk about Miah's passing, then maybe she could somehow keep the soul wrenching grief from surfacing again and maintain the façade that she'd moved on and was trying to live her best life. It wasn't true, but only she needed to know that. Everyone else just needed to keep their distance and she'd be fine. Once she could get back to her normal routine, that is.

. . ⌇⌇ . .

CHARITY WATCHED OVER Maddie while she slept, speaking peace into her mind and keeping the demons at bay. She'd watched and listened in as Maddie dealt with not being able to visit Miah's grave and the weekly phone call she refused to answer. She was surprised that Maddie hadn't become more emotional. Instead, she appeared to have just shutdown.

In the short term, that was actually a healthy move, considering the emotional rollercoaster Maddie had lived in this last year and some weeks. But in order for her to finally move forward in her life, she would have to deal with what happened and be willing to let go of her grief.

Maddie needed a good cry more than anyone Charity had ever met, but she held herself tightly in check. She guessed that was probably Maddie's way of maintaining control over a situation beyond her realm of influence. By not allowing herself to grieve, she not only didn't have to truly acknowledge her loss, but she could remain in control of herself in the midst of a situation that wanted to swallow her up like a blackhole. A hole that many people never returned from once they let go.

Charity was determined to help Maddie face her grief. Only then would her young charge be able to open her heart up to all of the love still in the world and see that she had a bright future ahead of her and wonderful memories of the past to rejoice in.

Chapter 4

The next morning...

Nick was having a bad morning. First, he'd discovered that he'd accidentally left the light on inside his car the night before and his battery was completely dead. He'd thought he wouldn't have to call for roadside assistance, since he'd found his electric battery jumper, but it hadn't been plugged in and was also completely dead. The tow company had arrived forty minutes after his phone call and had attempted to jump his battery, but it hadn't taken the jump and they'd needed to remove the battery and take it back with them to either refurbish or replace. They'd been kind enough to drive him to the hospital, but he was on his own for finding a ride back home.

That didn't bother him as much as the coffee stain that now decorated the front of his shirt. He'd paid a visit to the small coffee cart in the foyer of the hospital only to turn around and find himself smacking into a trash can he hadn't realized was there. His coffee had seemed to survive, but he hadn't noticed that the lid had come undone on one side and as he'd walked off the elevator and taken a sip, the entire contents of the cup had come pouring out and drenched the front of his shirt.

Normally, he would have retrieved the extra shirt he always kept in his trunk, but his trunk was currently located in the garage at his house. Ten miles away from the hospital. So, here he was, headed up to the third floor and hoping that the extra set of scrubs he'd ordered in his own size were still in the employee lounge. He'd decided to take the stairs, not wanting to run into anyone if he could possibly avoid it.

He stepped onto the third floor and then ducked into the employee lounge before any of the kids or staff could see him. He opened the locker with his name on it and smiled in relief at the stack of scrubs neatly folded inside. "I knew these would come in handy."

He grabbed the red pair on the top and then he grabbed a fresh towel and wash cloth from the stack on the linen rack. One of the features he appreciated most about this particular hospital was the accommodations that had been made for the employees. Each floor had their own lounge, complete with multiple bathroom stalls and at least two shower stalls. He stepped into the shower and quickly disrobed, pulling off his stained shirt and the white t-shirt he wore underneath. He shucked his dress slacks and then pushed everything out of the shower stall with his foot. He turned the water on, but instead of getting beneath the spray, he quickly used the washcloth to rinse the coffee from his person and then quickly dried off and got re-dressed.

He exited the employee lounge fifteen minutes later, ready for the day and hopefully some good news.

"Good morning, Teresa. How are the elves doing today?"

Teresa smiled, "Dr. Stavros, the elves are all doing fine, or was there one particular elf you were inquiring about?"

Nick frowned at her and then shook his head, "I'm concerned about all of my elves. After all, you ladies are the magic that helps my patients feel better."

"Thanks for that vote of confidence. As for the newest of the elves, she's around here somewhere."

"Well, then...I imagine I'll catch up to her at some point. See y'all in a bit." His Southern twang came out the most when he used certain words, and y'all was one of the worst. He frowned at the chuckle the ladies all had, having heard them talk about his Southern charm more than once when they thought he wasn't listening. Thankfully, everyone who worked on this ward, except the newest elf, was married. Happily. He didn't have to worry about being hit on by any of the nurses on the third floor and he didn't think his newest addition would be any different.

He grabbed the stack of charts waiting for him and headed down the hallway. He stopped at the second doorway and watched one of his favorite patient's struggling to lift a spoonful of orange Jell-O to her mouth.

He hurried forward, steadying her frail hand as she made it to her mouth and then smiled at him. "I'm glad to see your appetite is back, Sarah."

"I like orange Jell-O. The red stuff tastes like medicine, but the orange kind is okay. Do you want some? Maddie brought extra. She's really nice."

"Well, I'm glad to hear she's taking good care of you. And, no, I don't need any Jell-O right at the moment. I came by to check on you. Is your mom around?"

Sarah put down her spoon and then slowly shook her head. "Aunt Liza is here and dragged her down to the cafeteria. Mom didn't want to go, but Aunt Liza made her."

Sarah yawned and Nick nodded. "Why don't you lay back and close your eyes while I check things out and then we'll see about getting the rest of that Jell-O into your stomach?"

He picked up the bed's controller and eased it to a semi-flat position, watching Sarah's face for obvious signs of discomfort at the change of position. She was currently being treated for a tumor that had appeared on her kidney a month ago. The tumor had been malignant, and the kidney had been removed. Everything had been going well with her treatment until her remaining kidney had shown signs of failure three weeks ago.

The chemotherapy drugs and painkillers had taxed it beyond its capabilities and while Sarah was on her way to being declared "cancer free" for the moment, her kidney didn't look like it was going to recover. Nick had placed her on the transplant list five days ago and she was going to remain in the hospital until that time as she needed daily dialysis right now.

Nick listened to her lungs and her heart, pleased that everything sounded fine. He checked her temperature, only mildly concerned when it came back just shy of ninety-nine degrees. The chemotherapy drugs she'd been given were most likely responsible, but he made a note in her chart to have her lungs listened to at least twice every shift. He would rather be safe than sorry.

"Everything sounds good, kiddo." Sarah was only seven years old, but she knew more about how the human body worked than many first-year medical students. She was a bright little girl and had insisted he give her a thorough explanation for how the chemicals they were pumping into her body were going to help her.

Nick already knew that she would be insulted if he dumbed his explanation down, so he'd talked to her as if he was talking to another colleague and she'd surprised him by asking some very astute and pointed questions. Upon first diagnosing Sarah, he'd suggested they try to shrink the tumor with some targeted radiation therapy, in the hopes that the tumor could be removed, and the kidney salvaged.

Sarah had negated that by asking, "Will I be able to still have kids one day?"

Nick hadn't thought a seven-year old would be worried about that subject and had planned to let her parents know the long-term repercussions this type of radiation would have on her little body. He'd met her eyes and then slowly shook his head.

"Because we will need to use a high dose of radiation and it will be impossible to fully shield the ovaries from it, the likelihood of you being able to have children is very low."

He'd been impressed when the little girl, only six years old at the time, had looked at her parents and told them that God had promised she was going to be a mommy someday. Nick had been floored when her father had asked what the alternative was. After a lengthy discussion, and a night where Nick had probably spent as much time in prayer as the parents and child, the decision had been made to remove the kidney and treat with chemotherapy only.

Sarah had been a trooper these last weeks and it had been very hard for him to deliver the news about her remaining kidney, but Sarah and her parents had taken it all in stride. Their faith in God was evident for everyone to see and it had come at a time where Nick needed reminding that God was still there and He always would be, no matter how bad things were in the world.

"How's your pain level?" Nick asked, smiling when she opened her eyes and shrugged a shoulder.

"Okay. My back hurts when I move too fast."

"That's to be expected. I can increase your pain meds a tiny bit," he offered. Sarah shook her head, but he could tell she wasn't fully committed to that decision. He carefully sat on the chair next to her bed, bringing him down to her level and asked, "I know you don't like hurting, so why don't you want more pain medication?"

Sarah's little eyes filled with tears, and she tried in vain to sniff them back. Nick handed her a tissue and then waited for her to explain. She wiped her eyes and then gave him a weak smile. "I'm just being silly."

Nick hid his grin. The comment wasn't one you would expect to come from a seven-year old, but Sarah was an old soul trapped in a failing little girl's body and wise beyond her years. "Okay, so be silly. Tell me."

"The pain meds make me sleepy."

Nick nodded. "Yes, they can do that, but sleep is a good thing when you're not feeling well."

"But there's a magician coming this afternoon. I wanted to go..."

"So, why can't you go?" Nick asked. "You'll have to wear a mask because we can't risk you catching any unfriendly germs right now, but you can still go down and watch."

"Not if I'm sleeping." She covered up a yawn as she ended the statement and Nick mentally frowned. Sarah had nothing else to do but lie in bed, get her treatments, and rest. He'd been passing the dark circles beneath her eyes as a normal response to the trouble her body was having, but now he began to wonder...

"Sarah, did you sleep well last night?"

When she dropped her eyes, he knew he was on the right track. "Kiddo, why aren't you sleeping at night? Is it because you're in pain?"

Sarah swallowed and then nodded a little, "Some."

"So, the pain is partly what's keeping you awake." Nick pursed his lips and then cocked his head to the side. "What else is keeping you awake? Have you discovered some new television show that I don't know about? Something that I should be staying up to watch?"

When Sarah didn't answer him, he continued speaking, going for humor to draw her out. "I know, you've discovered that aliens are taking over the world, and they're secretly communicating with you through the television after everyone else goes to sleep."

Sarah shook her head, the hint of a smile playing around her lips. Nick continued, not willing to stop until she was giggling and had told him what was bothering her. As a physician, he knew the value of adequate sleep. No medication could replace the natural sleep that came when one willingly surrendered to fully relaxing.

"No? Okay. Let's see...," he stroked his imaginary beard and then held up a single finger. "I know...but, wait...no, that can't be it." He gave her a suspicious look and then looked at the side of her head, gingerly moving her chestnut curls back to reveal the top of her ear. He frowned and then shook his head, "No, I knew that wasn't it."

"Dr. Nick, tell me," Sarah told him with a smile. "What wasn't it?"

"No, sorry kiddo. I was just being silly."

"You said it was okay to be silly," she reminded him.

Nick smiled, "That I did. Okay, since you aren't talking to aliens, I thought maybe you were one of Santa's elves, sent here to check up on everyone and you were secretly talking to him at night, telling him who belongs on the 'Naughty' and 'Nice' list."

He looked sad and shook his head. "But that was just silly because your ears aren't pointed."

"Why are we talking about pointy ears?" Maddie asked as she pushed her way into the room with a food tray.

"Maddie! Dr. Nick thinks I'm one of Santa's elves and that's why I'm not sleeping at night," Sarah told her.

Nick watched Maddie digest the important part of her statement, and then play along. "Well, goodness, everyone on this floor knows you aren't one of Santa's elves. I should know," Maddie pointed to her own headband and the exaggerated elves ears sticking up through her hair. "After all, I came here directly from the North Pole."

Nick smiled at the way Maddie had so easily gained Sarah's trust. Maddie switched the food tray out, making sure to move the unfinished orange Jell-O and unopened containers to the new tray, and then she slowly sat Sarah back up. "Are you hungry?"

Sarah eyed the food and shook her head, "Not really."

Maddie nodded and then stuck a straw in the chocolate meal supplement. "How about you try drinking a bit of this and then we'll see how you feel about trying some mashed potatoes?"

Sarah dutifully nodded and took a sip. "It's good," she said in surprise. "What did you do? It always tastes kind of funny."

Maddie winked at her and then saw Nick watching her. She blushed a bit and explained in a loud whisper. "At the North Pole, we only like our chocolate milk really cold. I put it in the freezer for a bit."

"But it's not frozen," Sarah told her.

Maddie didn't miss a beat. "Well, no then it wouldn't be chocolate milk, but a chocolate popsicle."

"I like popsicles," Sarah told her with more enthusiasm than Nick had seen this morning.

He was about to make a suggestion, but Maddie was already way ahead of him. "In that case, I'll see what I can do to work some magic in the freezer. Now, want to tell me what's bothering you and keeping you from sleeping?"

Sarah's smile faltered, but Maddie didn't give her a chance to shut down. "I know you're not feeling great, or you wouldn't be in here. So, what kind of thoughts are going through that beautiful little brain and keeping you awake? Planning to take over the free world when you get out of here?"

Nick was amazed as how quickly Maddie had gotten to the heart of the matter. His patient was worried. In an adult or even an older child, he would have automatically addressed those concerns, but with Sarah...he had to remind himself that she didn't think like most seven-year old children.

"Are you worried, Sarah?"

She nodded. "What's going to happen?"

Maddie looked to Nick, and he took the reins back. "Well, you're going to get a new kidney. You'll be in the hospital for a few weeks and then you'll get to go home and heal up."

Sarah shook her head, "No, I know what's going to happen to me. But what about my mom? She seems so sad all of the time."

A gasp and muffled cry drew Nick and Maddie's eyes to the doorway where Sarah's mom and aunt had just returned. Maddie immediately jumped into action and ushered the two women from the room while Nick did his best to assure his little patient that everything was going to be fine.

"Your mom is just worried about you because you're very sick. She doesn't want anything else to happen to you. She's going to be fine, and she'll get all caught up on her sleep, when you do."

"Momma lost her job..."

"And she'll find another one once you're out of the hospital."

"My daddy told her it didn't matter and that everything was going to be fine, but she still cried."

Nick made a mental note to remind Sarah's parents that their brilliant little girl saw and heard everything. They needed to be a little more protective of her where adult matters were concerned. Nick assured Sarah that everything was going to be fine and then he wrote orders to increase her pain meds in the evening and also add a small amount of an anti-anxiety med to the mix.

"I'll stop by and check on you before the magic show. Don't worry, we'll get you something for the pain that won't make you sleepy."

"Promise?" Sarah asked him.

"Promise. Now, finish that chocolate milk Nurse Maddie made taste better and eat some of your potatoes. I'll send your mom and aunt in to help you when I see them."

He exited the room, frowning when he didn't see the two adults or Maddie. Teresa was nearby and he asked, "Did you see..."

"She took them down to the chapel. They haven't come out yet."

Nick nodded and then peeked in the window of the chapel. Sarah's mom was sobbing on her sister's shoulder while Maddie patted her hand. Since it looked like she had everything under control, he decided to wait and speak with them a little later. Right now, he had other patients needing his attention. He'd thank Maddie for her intuition and quick thinking later. Maybe he could even convince her to join him for dinner. She intrigued him and he found he really wanted to get to know her a bit better.

Chapter 5

Maddie sat quietly with the distraught mother and sister. She'd been through this same drill so many times in the past, but almost never when the patient was a delightful little girl that would eventually die unless someone else did first and gave her a new kidney. It was an ironic twist of fate for these parents that Maddie hadn't truly appreciated until now.

"Mrs. Thomas..."

"Please, call me Carol. This is my sister, Liza."

"Your husband?"

Carol shook her head and Liza reached over and squeezed her hand. "He's working...one of us has to." There was a level of desperation in her voice, but Maddie pushed it aside for the moment. No doubt there were many things at play in Carol's world, but Maddie wanted to focus on the concerns bothering her daughter first. Those were her primary concern.

Maddie smiled and squeezed her free hand. "Carol, I know what you're going through right now seems impossible. Dr. Stavros is taking excellent care of Sarah..."

"We know that." She exchanged a look with her sister. "It's just..., are we being selfish?" Carol asked. She pulled her hands free and fluttered them for a moment nervously before Liza reached out and hugged her.

"Selfish?" Maddie asked, already surmising what was bothering this mother.

"I can't even make myself pray the last few days," Carol cried. Tears filled her eyes and spilled over onto her cheeks as she struggled to maintain control of her emotions. "How can I pray for Sarah's new kidney when that means I'm praying for someone else's death?"

While these parents were praying for God to intervene and heal their children, they were also praying for a new organ to become available. At a gut level, that meant they were also praying for someone else to die. That was Sarah's mom's problem now. That and financial issues that were threatening to send the young family into medical bankruptcy in the midst of their daughters potentially lethal condition.

"Carol, you can't look at it that way. We don't see all sides of a story or a life, but God does. The chances that whoever is going to perish and provide Sarah's kidney is destined to die anyway, is very high."

Great advice, too bad you can't listen to yourself more often.

Maddie pushed aside her inner voice, ignoring her own jumbled emotions as she'd done for so many months, it had become her first response. She was becoming an expert at tending to others needs and offering them the moral and professional support her job demanded while keeping her own deficiencies and failures hidden. She was a nurse and helping both her patients and their families came with the territory.

"I just feel so...guilty," Carol told her, unaware of the thoughts running through Maddie's head.

"You have nothing to feel guilty over. How about we talk about something else for a minute?" Maddie suggested.

Carol wiped her eyes and nodded. "Sure. What would you like to talk about?"

"How about what you overheard Sarah telling Dr. Stavros and myself? Your daughter seems to think you're very sad lately."

"I guess I have been. I lost my job, and I can't help but wonder what's going to happen once she gets better and we leave here..."

"Sarah is picking up on your worries," Maddie told her as kindly as possible. "She's a unique little girl in that she sees and hears and understands so much more than other seven-year-olds. Right now, she needs to focus on getting her body strong enough so that once a kidney becomes available, she can go through the surgery and recover as quickly as possible. She's worried about you to the point that she's not sleeping at night."

Carol burst into a fresh bout of tears and Maddie rubbed her shoulder while Carol's sister tried to comfort her.

"I didn't mean...my husband and I were talking on the phone...I thought she was asleep..."

"It's okay, but now we need to make Sarah feels that you and your husband have everything under control so that she doesn't need to worry."

"You're talking about damage control?" Liza asked.

Maddie nodded slowly, "Yes, in a way. Your concerns are valid, they just don't need to be hers right now. Is your insurance covering her care here?"

"Most of it," Carol told her. "There's a daily co-pay and I don't know how we're going to pay that but..."

"Look, I'm going to set up a meeting with our finance office, if that's okay?" Maddie asked.

"What good would that do? They've been sending statements and the totals just keep growing."

"Trust me, you might be pleasantly surprised. We are a charity hospital which means we have a sliding fee scale for co-pays and the like. If you've lost your job since Sarah was first admitted here it might drastically change things as far as the hospital is concerned. It's worth a fifteen-minute meeting, isn't it?"

Carol wiped her tears and sat up straight, "Yes. Yes, I guess."

"It is. Let me call..."

"How about I just walk Carol over there right now and give her a chance to calm down? Sarah always seems to know when she's been crying," Liza suggested.

"I think that would be a good idea," Maddie smiled. "I'll let Sarah know you'll be back up to see her soon. Don't lose hope and please find someone to talk to when things get overwhelming. Anyone on this floor is willing to discuss things with you, or we have a wonderful chaplain service..."

"You've been helpful," Carol told her, hugging her tight and then giving her a watery smile. "I really do need that walk or Sarah will know the minute I walk in that I've been crying. I was never a pretty crier; my eyes get all puffy and my face gets blotchy."

"The finance office is on the other side of the hospital. If you're up for a short walk outside, you can cut through the parking area right beneath us and save yourself a lot of steps," Maddie offered.

"A brisk walk outside sounds like just the thing," Liza told her.

"Good. I'll see you both a little later then," Maddie touched Carol on the shoulder and then left the chapel area. She headed back to Sarah's room, oddly disappointed to see that Dr. Nick had already left and that Sarah appeared to be sleeping peacefully. She checked her chart and saw that the good doctor had not only added some additional pain medicine to her regimen, but a slight amount of anti-anxiety medication at night to help her sleep.

She grinned when she saw the note on the chart that instructed a nurse to wake Sarah up twenty minutes before the magic show this afternoon and to make sure she was taken down to the common room in plenty of time to socialize for a few minutes.

She closed out the note and then put a quick reminder in her phone. One of the other nurses might catch the note, but if not, Maddie would make sure Sarah got to see the magician herself. She left Sarah's room and headed back to the nurse's station. It was almost lunch time and she smiled perfunctorily at the others as she headed for the breakroom. She'd not had time to pack a lunch this morning, her entire routine feeling off, and she really wasn't up for a trip to the cafeteria. There were always so many people down there this time of day and her ability to hold it together was nearing empty. She just needed a chance to recharge, not have to pretend everything was going to be alright and try to get past the disjointed feeling that had been her constant companion since she woke up this morning and realized she couldn't go visit Miah. Dealing with Sarah's emotionally distraught mother hadn't helped.

She pulled out a chair and sat down, placing her hands on the table in front of her and pressing her palms to the cold, hard surface. She took several breaths, using the grounding technique – one of the few things she'd actually taken away from meeting with a grief counselor for so many weeks, after Miah's death. One breath. In. Out. Two breaths. In. Out.

She continued, closing her eyes as she forced her mind to go blank. She felt herself finally get to the place she wanted to go a few minutes later, and she floated there, no pain, no regrets, no sadness – just her, in touch with the table, breathing nice and even. The table was her anchor, it was stable, it didn't move, it didn't require anything from here, but it wasn't going anywhere. She continued to breath, forcing her muscles to soften.

She relaxed her shoulders and then moved that feeling throughout her body, so relaxed ten minutes into her exercise that she didn't even hear someone open the door and enter the lounge. Her first inclination that she was no longer alone was the whiff of masculine cologne, slightly tangy and woodsy, that forced her eyes open. Thankfully, Miah hadn't worn cologne, so she'd been spared having to relive losing him whenever she encountered someone who did.

She sniffed slowly, liking the smell and how it blended with the man's natural smells...*Man?*

Maddie opened her eyes. There weren't any male nurses working on this floor, so who was in the employees' lounge? She looked over her shoulder and felt her stomach do a little flip as she spied Dr. Nick Stavros standing at the small kitchenette, fixing himself a cup of coffee. He didn't turn around, but he seemed to know when she had.

"Feeling better?" he asked, stirring creamer into his cup.

Maddie cleared her throat and asked softly, "Better? Was I feeling bad?"

He turned then and stared at her, his eyes seeing everything. "You tell me? You were grounding yourself. Why?"

Chapter 6

M addie flushed and looked down at where her forearms and palms were still pressed to the tabletop. She pulled them toward her, breaking the contact and immediately felt her anxiety begin to rise again. She frowned and then mentally shoved the feelings away. *I can do this. Get up and go to the cafeteria and get away from this conversation. Now.*

She pushed up from the table and gave him a forced smile she hoped looked natural, "I was just resting for a moment before I headed down to get lunch."

He arched a brow at her, making himself look even more handsome and dangerous. His dark hair and dark eyes, set in a classic face that was tanned from being outdoors, was the type of face you expected to see on a model for hiking boots or climbing gear. It was down-to-earth, but also so heart-stopping gorgeous it was hard to look away. *No wonder so many of the women here are after him. The man is lethal without even trying.*

"Lunch sounds good. I think I'll join you," he told her, taking a sip of his coffee and then closing his eyes in delight. "Good, but I need food."

He opened the door and then looked at her and gestured with his head, "Coming?"

"I..." Maddie was at a loss for how to handle this situation. She'd backed herself into a corner by telling him what she was planning to do, even though it hadn't actually been true. Then he'd invited himself along, and now she felt stuck.

"You know, I'm not really feeling all that hungry," she hedged. "I might just grab a power bar or something from the vending machine..."

"Nonsense. Working up here takes a lot out of a person and you need to refuel. Besides, I wanted a chance to talk to you about earlier. We'll make it a working lunch," he gave her that charming smile and she could easily imagine most women would fall at his feet to do his bidding when he turned on the charm.

Feeling backed into a corner, she nodded and preceded him from the room. Teresa and Ciera were coming down the hallway and he boldly informed them, "Nurse Maddie and I are headed downstairs to the cafeteria. You girls can hold down the fort, can't you?"

"Of course," Teresa smiled at them both.

Ciera nodded and then asked Maddie, "Bring me back one of those cinnamon rolls, would you?"

"Sure," Maddie nodded, feeling like she was caught in a time warp. She'd only spoken to the other nurse a few times, and yet she was going to bring her back food. She could do that, it just seemed odd since Maddie normally kept her distance from her co-workers whenever possible.

"We'll be back in under an hour."

Maddie gave Teresa and Ciera a look that begged for help, but they simply smiled serenely at her and gave her a thumb's up. *No help coming from that direction.*

He was holding the elevator for her when she caught up to him. She mumbled,

"Thanks," she mumbled, catching up to him and the elevator.

"No problem. So how do you like working up here so far?"

"It's only my second day," she reminded him.

"Yeah, so?" he arched another brow and she forced herself not to notice how handsome he was.

"It's very different but in so many good ways."

"Great. That's what I like to hear. These kids spend so much of their childhoods in and out of hospitals, I really wanted to create an environment that seemed friendlier and less rigid. Less hospital like and more like a trip to camp."

Maddie nodded as the elevator doors opened. Once again, she preceded him out and then turned to her left. The cafeteria was bustling. Thankfully, she was able to move about and get her own food without having to maintain any further conversation with him. It was just her misfortune to get in line to check out right behind Jamie.

"Hey, girl. How's working up on the peds floors? And what on earth are you wearing?" Jamie asked, eyeing her pink scrubs with nutcrackers, ballet dancers, and Christmas trees scattered over them.

"Peds is fine, and these are scrubs," Maddie told her, resisting the urge to turn around and locate Dr. Nick.

"I haven't been on that floor in a while, but if those scrubs are any indication of what it's like to work up there, sign me up," Jamie told her with a bright grin. "Wow," she murmured, looking over Maddie's shoulder.

Maddie didn't even have to turn around to know what Jamie was looking at, his cologne announced him.

"Is that all you're eating?" he asked, eyeing her plate of French fries and bowl of fresh fruit.

She turned to look at him and his tray, her eyes going wide at how much food was piled upon it. "You're going to eat all of that? For lunch? How do you not weigh four hundred pounds?" she asked before she could even consider how personal the comment might seem to someone – like Jamie, who was avidly listening in.

"I have a rather high metabolism and I plan to work it off on the racquetball court later." He tipped his head toward Jamie and lowered his voice, "A friend of yours."

Maddie followed his look and saw the questioning look on Jamie's face and cringed. "Oh, sorry. Jamie, this is Dr. Stavros. Jamie and I used to work together on the second floor."

Nick gave Jamie a smile and nodded at her. "Nice to meet you."

"Doctor, I can ring you up over here," one of the cafeteria clerks announced, opening up a second checkout lane.

"Great." He picked up his tray and then reached for hers, taking it with him to the other lane before she could even protest. "Nice to meet you, Jamie," he said. "I'll grab us a table so that you two can finish your conversation."

Maddie nodded, feeling Jamie's eyes boring into her skull. "I should probably..."

"Explain. Now. You're having lunch with Dr. Hottie?"

"That's not his name," Maddie told her.

"No, but that's how everyone thinks of him. The man is not only single, but genuinely nice and smart and handsome...Do I need to go on?"

"He runs the third floor, and I was headed for lunch and he just decided to join me," Maddie told her by way of explanation.

"Girl, why don't you seem happy about that fact? There are women working here who would gladly give their right arm to have him smile at them, let alone want to spend any time alone with them."

Maddie snorted as she glanced around. "We're hardly alone and I'm going to eat my fries and go back to work. You should do the same thing." She shook her head at Jamie and then excused herself and went to find said French fries and the good doctor who had absconded with them. She found him in a corner booth, already digging into the mound of food on his plate.

She took a seat opposite him and then watched him eat for a moment before she shook her head and put some ketchup on her plate. "You're going to end up being a patient here if you keep eating like that."

"I don't eat like this all of the time, but this morning was hectic and filled with one disaster after another." He paused and when she didn't say anything, he continued, "What disaster, you asked? Well, first my car wouldn't start. The battery's dead and the service truck took a long time to get there. Then I stopped for coffee in the lobby but ended up dumping the entire contents on my shirt as I got off the elevator. Since my extra clothes are in the trunk of my car, which doesn't happen to be anywhere close to the hospital, I changed into scrubs. That all happened before I'd been awake even two hours."

"Sounds like your morning wasn't dull," Maddie commented, popping a fry drenched in ketchup into her mouth.

He eyed her and then went back to eating. They did that in silence for a few minutes and then he paused and put his fork down. "I wanted to thank you for your quick response with Sarah's mom and aunt earlier. Sarah isn't your typical seven-year-old and sees and hears everything."

"I got that the first time I talked with her. She's an old soul inside that tiny body."

"Yeah, and unfortunately, the stress is getting to her mom. Carol normally keeps it together pretty well, but with the holidays fast approaching things seem like they are getting a bit too much for her to handle."

Maddie shook her head and finished chewing before saying, "I don't think that's what's fueling her anxiety as much as knowing that in order for Sarah to get a new kidney, someone else has to die."

Nick shook his head, "I didn't even think of that. Carol would most definitely be thinking about that kind of thing. So, were you able to make any headway with her?"

"Maybe. The sister, Liza, she gets it. There were also some concerns about the hospital fees. Now that Carol isn't working, they can barely afford to pay their regular bills and the idea of owing the hospital thousands of dollars was freaking her out."

"I hate this part of medicine."

Maddie nodded and then told him about directing them to the finance office and the new programs they might qualify for.

"Thank you for doing that. Working with peds is different because we have to care for the parents almost as much as the patients. You seem to have a great rapport with the kids and staff. And the parents have been raving about what a good choice was made in bringing you on board up there."

Maddie flushed at the praise and went back to eating her food.

"No comment?"

"Not really."

"How did you know to freeze the meal supplement drink?"

"Well, it just kind of made sense. Most of the patients complain because it has an after taste and is slightly gritty. Cooling it down seems to get rid of that taste and the thicker it gets the less bothersome the texture becomes. I really am going to try freezing some of it."

"If you find some popsicle holders, you know those reusable plastic kind?" he asked.

"My mom had some when I was a kid," Maddie told him with a smile. "I bet I can find some at a local big box store, or there's always Amazon."

"Well, if you find some, buy a couple sets and then give Teresa the receipt."

"Why would I do that?"

"Because anything that benefits the kids on my ward becomes a hospital expense. Trust me, they've never turned down a receipt. It's part of the deal I have with the hospital. I stay here and offer the best pediatric oncology treatment in this part of the United States, and they leave the third floor alone. Entirely."

"How does that work?" Maddie asked. "I mean, it's all part of the hospital, isn't it?"

"It is, but aside from handling the normal paperwork, what actually happens on the third floor is entirely up to me. Hence, the scrubs, the decorations, the daily activities and parties. Those are all diversionary tactics to help get the kids' minds off their pain and treatments and diagnoses. An attempt to give them back a part of their childhood that has been stolen by disease and illness."

Maddie felt tears sting her eyes as she listened to his impassioned speech. It was obvious that Dr. Nick Stavros cared deeply for his patients and was willing to do whatever it took to help them fight and win the battle. She started to give voice to her thoughts, but his pager went off.

"Sorry." He glanced at it and then frowned. "I've got to take this. How about we finish this discussion over dinner? Tonight? My treat?"

"Uhm..."

He picked up his tray and then eyed her, "I really could use a ride home and I'd like to get to know you a bit better. So, dinner? Please?"

Maddie couldn't believe he was practically begging, and she laughed when he gave her sad puppy dog eyes. "Fine. Just, don't look at me like that. I'll be accused of being mean to everyone's favorite doctor."

"Do tell?" His pager went off again and he shook his head, "Correction, you can tell me all about that later. I'm needed in surgery. I'll find you on the floor at the end of your shift."

Maddie nodded bemused as he almost sprinted to the tray drop off and then bolted from the cafeteria.

Chapter 7

She directed her attention back to her own plate while noticing that several employees seated around the cafeteria had witnessed their exchange and were now giving her speculative looks.

Great! Now I'll be the focus of the hospital gossip line.

With her appetite gone, she dumped her own tray and then took the stairs back up to the third floor. She didn't realize it until that moment but having lunch with Nick had done more for helping ground her than any exercise she'd ever done. It seemed that all she'd needed today was to focus on the here and now and she was already feeling stronger and more capable of finishing out the day with her customary attention to detail.

She stepped onto the floor and almost collided with Teresa who was rushing down the hall toward Zachary's room. "What's going on?"

"Zachary's not doing very well."

Maddie joined her, both of them stopping to glove and mask up before entering the little boy's room. His color was even more off today and he seemed to be having trouble taking a full breath. Teresa checked his IV and Maddie went to his bedside and took his pulse.

"Hey, Zach. Are you in more pain today?"

"It hurts when I ...when I...breathe."

Maddie shared a concerned look with Teresa and pulled out her stethoscope to listen to his chest. He had slight raspy sounds on his right side, and she gave Teresa a worried look. "We might need a chest x-ray, just to be on the safe side."

Teresa nodded and left the room to go put in the order. Maddie turned her attention back to Zach and adjusted the angle of his bed, pleased when it seemed to help his breathing momentarily. "Are you hurting?"

"Not much, just when I try to breathe deep or cough. I don't like coughing, it really hurts," he told her sadly.

Maddie snagged a chair with her ankle and sat down beside him. "I know, buddy. How about I stay with you for a bit, just until they get here with the x-ray machine, and we make sure your lungs are playing nice in the sand box."

"Lungs can't play in sandboxes," he told her with a look that said she should have known that.

"I know, it's just an expression meaning your lungs are supposed to be staying healthy and they might not be doing such a good job of that."

"Does that mean I'm going to die?" Zach asked without inflection in his voice.

"It means that if your lungs are getting an infection, we'll give you some medicine to make it go away."

"I'm not afraid to die," he told her.

"You're not?" she asked, not sure where this conversation was going.

"No. My daddy's in heaven. Nick said so. He's waiting for me, but he wants me to grow big and become an adult before I go see him."

Maddie tried not to tear up and nodded. "I'm sure your daddy is looking down and hoping you get all better."

Miah, are you looking down on me?

She had tried not to let herself think that way, but now that the thought had entered her mind, she couldn't seem to get rid of it.

"...play baseball?"

Maddie brought her mind back to the present and shook her head at the hopeful look on Zach's face. "I'm sorry, kiddo. What did you ask me?"

"Do you think I'll be strong enough to play baseball?"

Maddie blinked several times and then answered as best she could. "Well, let's see. It's December now and baseball season doesn't usually get started until April, so if you keep getting stronger there's a good possibility."

"Good. I never got to play baseball. Nick said he'd help me get signed up if I keep getting better."

"Well, there you go then. Sounds like I might have to come see a few baseball games."

"You'll come watch me play?" Zach asked.

"I'd love to," Maddie assured him. It would actually kill her to be at a ballpark. Miah had been their high school team's star catcher, and she'd spent hours behind home plate watching him play the game he loved. She swallowed back the emotions that flooded her and, when she lost the battle with holding back her tears, she stood up and told Zach, "I'll be back in just a minute."

She ducked into the hallway and then walked to the nearest storage room and stepped inside. Once the door was closed, she bent her knees, wrapping her arms around her chest and gave way to the tears that wouldn't stop. She buried her head in her arms and, for several long moments, she just let the grief flow over her. It wasn't something she allowed very often and had never allowed while she was at work. It often wiped her out. After several moments, the worst was over. She wiped her cheeks and tried to figure out how she was going to get through the remainder of her shift.

She took an extra few minutes and then blew her nose and forced a smile to her face as she opened the storage room and stepped out. She wasn't expecting to see Nick standing across the hallway, waiting for her with a questioning look on his face. She turned to her right, away from Zach's room, but Nick's voice stopped her.

"You're not going to go back in there and finish your discussion with Zach about baseball?"

She shook her head and gave him a dismayed look. "I thought you were needed in surgery?"

"False alarm." He nodded at the closet. "Zach told me all about your conversation and then said you got this sad look on your face and left the room in a hurry. Want to tell me what's going on?'

"No," Maddie told him boldly. "I'll talk to him for a minute more and then I need to check on some other patients."

She skirted around him, ignoring his narrowed assessing gaze, popped her head into Zach's room and then walked over to the bedside. "Sorry about that, buddy. You still doing okay?"

"The x-ray person came. Dr. Nick says I have pneumonia."

"Just a little start and we'll take care of that with some antibiotics," Nick said over her shoulder.

"You'll be breathing easier in no time," she told Zach. "I'm going to go check on some other kids. Do you want me to bring you anything when I come back? Jell-O? Ice cream?"

"Can I have one of those yellow popsicles?" Zach asked.

"I'll see what I can come up with." She straightened up his covers and then laid a hand on his shoulder, "Hang in there, okay."

She gave Nick a cursory glance and then left the room, heading straight for the employees' lounge where she quickly washed her face and forced herself to lock her emotions away once more.

The rest of the afternoon went by very quickly. The magician showed up right on time, and all of the children were able to attend, even Sarah and Zach. Maddie didn't actually talk to Nick again, even though she saw him watching her several times as she interacted with the children, having been selected by the magician to be his assistant.

She played it up for the children's sake, being overly dramatic and earning smiles of approval from parents and staff members alike. It was just the medicine she needed to get her mind off her earlier upset, and she completed the last two hours with a smile on her face that wasn't as forced as before.

She was just finishing her patient notes when Nick spoke behind her. "Ready to get out of here?"

"Just about," she told him quietly. "About dinner..."

"Not up to it tonight?" he asked, eyeing her once again critically.

"Not really. It's been kind of a long day."

"I hear that. How about we hit a fast food drive thru and you can either eat with me at my place, or just take your food home with you?"

"I guess..."

"Great. Change and I'll meet you down in the lobby. I need to say goodnight to Zach."

She watched him walk away, far too aware of how good he looked in his street clothes and mad at herself because she kept noticing. Penny sidled up next to her and whispered, "You and the doc got a hot date tonight?"

Maddie shook her head, a little too emphatically to be believable. "His car wouldn't start this morning and I'm taking him home." When Penny's eyebrows went up, Maddie hurried to correct her wording. "To his house. I'm taking him home to his house."

"I get it. No problem," Penny smirked and then walked away whistling.

Maddie sighed and then headed to change out of her scrubs. She tossed them in the dirty clothes basket, pleased that she didn't have to add laundry to her chore list tonight. She grabbed her gloves and took the stairs down to the foyer. Nick was talking with the security guard when she arrived and stopped to watch her walk toward him, making her very self-conscious in the process.

"Ready to go?" she asked softly, needing to break the tension that seemed to be building between them.

"Sure thing. George, see you tomorrow."

"Have a goodnight, Dr. Stavros. Maddie. How you doing, girl?"

Maddie swallowed and nodded. "I'm okay, George."

"You sure? I talked to my brother-in-law yesterday and he said you're still going out to the cemetery twice a day. Girl, it's been over a year. What's going on?"

Maddie began to panic when she realized Nick was listening intently to their conversation. "I'm fine. Really. I need to get Dr. Stavros home. See you tomorrow."

She turned away, knowing she was bordering on being rude, but she couldn't do this today. Not today. Probably not tomorrow, either. She headed for her vehicle with Nick by her side. He gratefully waited until they were out of the parking lot before he asked about her conversation with George.

"Cemetery?"

"It's nothing," she told him, keeping her eyes straight forward.

"Didn't sound like nothing. George seemed very concerned about you. Anything you want to talk about?"

"No."

"No?" he queried back. He was silent for a long moment and then asked, "Is this something you've ever talked about?"

They were at a stoplight and Maddie turned to look at him. "I don't need to talk to anybody. I already did that, for all the good that it did me. That's where I learned the grounding techniques you saw me using earlier. They don't always work, but today...well, it's been an unsettling day. I'm fine. I'm handling things just fine."

The light turned green, and she spied a popular Mexican fast food place up ahead. She put her blinker on and then asked, "Is this okay?"

"Fine."

After they ordered food, she asked, "What part of town do you live in?"

He gave her an address and she frowned. It was only about a block away from her apartment. "Do you need directions?"

"No. I live in the Crestwood Apartments."

"Really? We're practically neighbors," he told her with a smile, snagging a chip from his bag.

Maddie nodded and then drove in silence until she reached his driveway.

"It looks like they returned your battery," she nodded toward the front door where it was sitting in plain sight beneath the porch light.

"Great. Guess I won't need to bum a ride into work tomorrow, after all. Sure you won't come in and eat with me?"

"No. It's been a long day. Thank you for lunch and dinner," she told him.

"That is has been and you're very welcome. I am going to treat you to an actual dinner at a restaurant one day soon. Have a good evening." He got out of the car with his dinner bag in hand. She waited until his front door was open before she drove off.

At her apartment, she ate her food, watched some television absentmindedly for an hour, and then crawled into bed. She kept her mind turned off, refusing to allow her emotions to surface again. If the third floor continued to be this crazy, she wasn't sure how she'd survive. Not without having a complete emotional breakdown and finally being forced to face what she'd been hiding from for over a year.

That was simply unacceptable.

Chapter 8

Several days later...

Maddie's head was killing her. She thought she'd been doing a good job of concealing her pain, until she visited Zachary's room. The little boy saw right through her forced smile and stilted questions.

"What's wrong with your eye?" he asked.

Maddie frowned and then realized her left eye was twitching a bit. It was a common occurrence when she was headed for a massive migraine and she blamed her lack of sleep and the disruption to her schedule.

I'm going to the cemetery after work, locked gate or not.

"I just have a little headache today," she told him quietly. She adjusted his new IV bag and spotted a drawing pad open in front of him alongside a small pile of pencils. "What are you drawing?"

"My dad," Zach said in a quiet voice.

Maddie peered at the pad and took in the details. The man was a bigger image of Zach, in his military uniform, and the drawing was very well done. "That's really good, Zach."

He nodded and then pulled out a picture from beneath the drawing pad, showing his dad in uniform with the American flag and the military flag behind him. "This is him. He died."

Maddie swallowed and then nodded. "I heard. I'm sorry."

Zach nodded and then looked up at her. "Have you ever had anybody die?"

The question was asked so simply, and Maddie stared at him for a long moment as tears started to form in her eyes. She wanted to lie and just walk away, but Zach was obviously trying to find someone who might understand what he was going through. She knew how badly loss felt, she lived each and every day. She could no more deny him the opportunity to realize he wasn't alone, than she could deny him proper medical care.

She sank down into the bedside chair and nodded. "I have."

"Your parents?" Zach asked.

Maddie shook her head, "No. My fiancé was killed just like your dad was. He was in the military."

Zach reached over and laid his hand over her larger one. "I'm sorry. It hurts. Really bad. There are times when I really want to talk to him. To tell him what's happening to me, but he's not there and he's never coming back." Tears slid down his cheeks and Maddie realized she was crying as well.

She stood up and sat on the edge of his bed, crossing a line she'd held for over a year, and hugged his little body close, being cognizant of the IVs and other monitoring devices he was hooked up to. "I know, buddy."

"Nick says it's okay to be sad and that crying is healthy."

"He does, does he?"

I disagree. Crying doesn't solve anything. I should know. I've spent the last year crying, and it still hurts as much now as it did the day I found out.

"I don't like to cry," Zach told her.

She sniffed back tears and then asked, "Why not?"

"Because babies cry. My dad never cried."

"Oh, I'm sure he probably did, he just didn't want you to know because he was supposed to be the parent and be the strong one."

Zach thought about that for a moment, wiping his tears with the back of his hands. "He was really sad when he found out I had cancer."

"I bet he was. Especially because he couldn't come home to take care of you."

"That's why he called Nick. To take care of me while he was gone."

"I'm glad Dr. Nick was able to go get you and bring you here."

"Me too." Zach was quiet for a long time and then asked, "What's going to happen once I get better?"

Maddie dried her eyes and sat back, looking at him to see what he was really asking. "You mean, what kind of activities will you be able to do?"

Zach shook his head. "No. Where am I gonna live? Grandma doesn't want me."

"Wait. Why would you think that? Your grandma came out here with you."

"But then she left. She said her other daughter and grandchildren needed her and that I had plenty of people taking care of me. She just left one day and didn't even say goodbye."

Maddie's heart broke at the sadness on his face. "Zach, Dr. Nick said your grandmother was having some memory issues. She was having trouble remembering things. I'm sure she didn't mean to leave without saying goodbye. Have you talked to her since she left?"

"Once. She called me on my birthday, but she couldn't talk very long because she was at Justin's football game."

"Justin is your cousin?"

"Yeah. He's sixteen and plays quarterback. He's really good."

"Do you like football?" Maddie asked, glad the emotions of a few minutes ago were beginning to calm down. She truly didn't want to get into the discussion about where Zachary was going after he left the hospital. It seemed as if Dr. Nick wanted to become his guardian, but Maddie wasn't sure of that and refused to say anything that might get the little boy's hopes up.

"Yeah, but I don't like watching by myself." Zach sat up a bit in his bed and then gave her a sly look. "There's a game tonight. Wanna watch with me?"

Maddie could see the yearning in his eyes and started to say "no," but then realized she really didn't want to go home to her empty apartment again. It was in the single digits outside so even if she walked to Miah's gravesite, she wouldn't be able to stay out there for very long without getting frostbite. Watching a football game with Zach seemed like a much better option.

Another thought occurred to her and she gave him a sideways look. "You know, I kind of have a routine when I watch football games at night."

"What is it?" Zach asked with enthusiasm.

Maddie smiled and then whispered, "Pizza."

"Pizza?" Zach whispered back.

"Yeah. With lots of gooey cheese."

"And pepperoni?" Zach asked with wide eyes.

"Lots of pepperoni," Maddie exaggerated the words. "I don't know if I could watch a game without pizza. But...well, do you like pizza?"

Zach nodded his head and then the light died in his eyes and he looked incredibly sad. "I can't leave the hospital and the pizza here is yucky."

Maddie had tried the pizza once, only once, and she full-heartedly agreed. It was one of the few items the cafeteria didn't do well. "How about I order a pizza, and have it delivered here? I could maybe watch the game with you?"

In reality, Maddie used to love football. So had Miah. She hadn't watched a game since his death and she almost regretted making the offer, but the happiness on his face would be worth every minute of pain she had to endure. Zach had lost so much, and he was so young...to lose both parents...tonight would be a small price to pay to put a smile on his face.

"Will you get in trouble?" Zach asked.

"For ordering pizza? No. Luckily, you can eat anything your little heart desires."

"It wants pizza," Zach told her in a very decisive voice.

"Then pizza it shall have. I need to go finish my shift, but I'll be back a little after five o'clock. What time does the game come on?"

"Six o'clock."

"I'll be back before that. Do you need anything else before I leave?" Maddie asked, checking his equipment one last time.

"No. You promise you'll come back?" Zach asked with worry in his voice.

Maddie leaned over and kissed his forehead. "I promise." She winked at him and then let herself out of his room. She took a few steps and then turned around and walked to the window at the end of the hallway and looked out over the skyline. It was snowing again, and she tried to focus on the falling flakes while doing her best to keep her emotions in check.

God, I probably have no right to ask this of you, but these children...they are hurting, and their parents are so scared. I don't know why you put me on this floor, I can barely make it an entire shift without almost breaking down. Haven't we all suffered enough?

Anyway, could you help them? Build up Zach's strength. Help Sarah hang in there until a new kidney is found. Thanks.

After several long moments, she finally pulled it together enough to finish her shift. She visited with Sarah and her mother for a short while, assuring Carol that Sarah's name was moving up the transplant list as quickly as possible.

They were making ornaments out of popsicle sticks, red pom poms, googly eyes, pretzels, and Elmer's glue when she walked past the common area. Dr. Nick was sitting right in the middle of the space, laughing and giggling with the kids as they tried to create their own versions of the Rudolph ornament. Teresa and Sheila had joined in on the fun as well, and Maddie found it impossible to not smile at the joy on everyone's faces.

"Nurse Maddie, come make an ornament with us?" Melanie called out. The little girl had gotten the news that a match had been found for her upcoming bone marrow transplant. The surgery would be taking place in five days and everyone was hoping she might be able to go home for Christmas shortly thereafter. She'd be on immunosuppression drugs for months, if not longer, but the success rate with bone marrow transplants and ridding the body of leukemia were rising every day.

"How about you make one for me?" Maddie called back.

"Okay," the young girl called back.

Maddie continued on down the hall, entering Paula's room quietly to hang another bag of IV fluid and to change out the morphine pump. Paula had a rare form of brain cancer and had been fighting valiantly for almost a year, but nothing seemed to be working in the last few months. She'd had all of the surgery they could offer, chemotherapy, and even radiation, but instead of the tumor shrinking, it had begun to grow again, and she'd been given the worst news possible. They were out of options for treatment and without a bonified miracle from heaven, she would most likely very soon.

For most cancer patients, their immune systems simply didn't work like their peers. Paula was no different. She'd been brought back to the hospital a week before Maddie started working on the floor with a small cold. Within a day, she'd been fighting off pneumonia and a whole slew of other complications a healthy child would never experience. For a child with a compromised immune system like Paula's, a common cold could kill.

Paula's father was sleeping in the companion bed and Maddie gently touched his shoulder and gestured for him to follow her out into the hallway. She partially closed the door and then asked, "How's she doing?"

"The pain seems to be under control better today. I'm Brian, by the way."

Maddie gave him a small smile. "Brian, I'm Maddie. Dr. Stavros increased her dosage. Is there anything I can get you?"

"No." He paused and then stated boldly, "Her mother went home to get her brother and bring him up here."

Maddie heard the unspoken *to say goodbye* and cleared her throat while she thought of something else to say. Paula's father gave her a sad nod and then breathed out heavily. "I should get back in there..."

She reached out and laid a hand on his shoulder. "She's a fighter. Please, if there's anything anyone of us here on the floor can do for you, please...just let us know."

"We will. You all have been wonderful. We couldn't have asked for better care for our daughter." He was becoming more emotional the longer they talked. "I just wish…" He started to break down and then caught himself. "Sorry."

Maddie gave him a sad smile. "You don't ever have to apologize to me or anyone else working on this floor." She walked over and then pushed the door to the room back open and whispered, "Someone will be back to check on her in a bit."

"Thank you." Brian swallowed and then forced a smile to his lips as he re-entered the room. Maddie followed him and quickly took the young girl's vitals and recorded them on the electronic charting laptop in the corner.

Maddie left Paula's room and realized she only had a few minutes of her shift left. She was emotionally spent today. She was looking forward to relaxing and doing something more normal this evening. She spent them updating her patient files, and then she clocked out and headed for the employee lounge. She changed into her street clothes, pulled out her phone and located a nearby pizza parlor that offered delivery.

"Paolo's Pizzeria."

"Yes, uhm…I was wondering, do you deliver to the hospital?" Maddie asked the voice on the phone.

"Sure do. If you give me the floor and room number, we can bring it right to you."

"Great. I need a large pepperoni pizza, napkins, plates, and some packets of parmesan cheese."

"Okay. Anything else?"

"No, that will do it." Maddie gave him her credit card information and the room number for the delivery driver. She then called down to the security desk and told them what was happening. She grabbed a couple of sodas from the kitchen and headed for Zachary's room. She had a football game to watch and a little boy to make smile.

Chapter 9

Charity couldn't believe how things were progressing with Maddie. She hovered in the corner of Zachary's room and watched as Maddie and the eight-year-old whooped for a good play and hollered at the officials on the television screen when they objected to a call. As a guardian angel, she truly didn't understand the game where human adult men tackled one another, and thousands of other humans paid money to go and watch them.

When the game had first started, Charity had been concerned that Maddie would chicken out and not stick around to watch the game. Then Zachary had hugged her, tears in his eyes because she'd kept her word to come back. Maddie's heart had softened, and she'd settled in for the duration.

It was just after the half time of the game and Zachary was starting to get tired, but he didn't want to go to sleep just yet.

"I heard there was a party going on down here and I wasn't invited?" Dr. Nick asked as he came into the room.

"Nick! Maddie bought pizza!" Zach exclaimed with a broad smile.

"Pizza!" Nick looked at her as he came into the room. "From downstairs?"

Zach make a gagging sound and Maddie chuckled. "No. Gross."

"Well, that's kind of what I was thinking but didn't want to insult Nurse Maddie's choices."

"I don't feel insulted. In fact, I should probably scoot out of here and let Zach get some sleep."

"But, Maddie," Zach whined. "The game's not over yet."

"Yeah, Nurse Maddie," Nick chimed in with a smile. "The game's not over yet."

Maddie looked at both boys and Charity chuckled at the look she gave the wall where they couldn't see. Maddie huffed out a breath and then sat back down. "Fine. It's almost the fourth quarter anyway."

"Great," Nick told her, snagging another chair and setting it down right beside her own. "I'm off shift so I'll just watch the rest of the game with you. Who's playing tonight?"

"The Seahawks and Vikings," Zach offered. "The Vikings are stomping Seattle all over field."

"There's pizza left," Maddie told him, "Help yourself."

Nick gave her a charming smile and slipped a slice from the box. "Thanks. Not sure how I feel about the Vikings having the upper hand, but then again, there's...six minutes left. A lot can happen in six minutes."

"A lot can happen in six minutes," Maddie murmured. Charity felt her forcibly push past memories aside. She wasn't sure if it was because they were bittersweet or just too painful to deal with.

They all settled down and returned to watching the game as Charity observed them. Nick kept glancing at Maddie, but she was sitting ramrod straight, keeping her eyes straight forward. Almost as if she was afraid to look at Nick.

Charity found that very interesting and moved a bit closer to Nick, hoping to pick up on his emotions. She sensed that Nick was intrigued by Maddie. Now that she was tuned into both adults' thoughts, she settled in the corner to listen and hopefully learn what she needed to help Maddie move forward with her life. Christmas was coming and Charity was running out of time.

"So, who do you want to win?" Nick asked.

"The Seahawks," Zach immediately spoke up. "Maddie, who do you want to win?"

"It doesn't really matter to me, I don't really get into football these days," Maddie murmured.

"Meaning you used to? What changed?" Nick asked.

Maddie shook her head, hating herself for even hinting that she had a past. "Nothing." She pretended to yawn, needing a valid excuse to go home without hurting Zach's feelings. "Hey, kiddo, I'm not going to stay for the end of the game since Dr. Nick's here with you. I didn't sleep very well last night..."

Zach's face fell and his lower lip quivered. "Please?" Charity started to intervene, but moments later her help wasn't needed. Zach reached out and grabbed hold of her sleeve. "Please, Maddie?"

Maddie made the mistake of looking into Zach's eyes and caved. "But who needs sleep. I'll stay."

"Obviously, not you," Nick whispered for her ears only.

She ignored him and sat back down next to Zach, earning a warm smile. When Zach loosened his grip on her sleeve and reached down, covering her hand with his own, another small piece of her heart became his. She turned her palm over and clasped his small hand within hers and they finished watching the game that way.

Thirty minutes later, the game ended with the Vikings getting the win. "Sorry, Zach. Guess your team just wasn't playing their best tonight," Maddie told him, ruffling his hair.

Zach grinned and then laughed. "That's okay, the Vikings are a better team, but purple? I mean, that's a girl color."

Maddie and Nick both laughed at that announcement and shook their heads. "Don't let those big linebackers hear you say that."

"I happen to have a purple shirt," Nick offered. "I believe the clerk at the store called it eggplant, but really...it's purple."

"And you wear it?" Zach asked with wide eyes.

"I've been told it makes my eyes stand out," Nick told him cheekily.

"Ew. A girl told you that."

"How do you know that?" Maddie inquired as she began to clean up the room and dispose of their trash. She forced herself not to look at Nick or imagine what he would look like wearing a deep purple shirt. His eyes would definitely be hard to look away from then.

"Guys don't talk about other guy's eyes," Nick was explaining to his young patient.

"Well, there is that," Maddie agreed, tossing away their plates and busying herself in the corner. "How about I help you back into your bed and I go get your night pain meds?"

Zach's face had gone ashen ten minutes before the game ended and Maddie had been carefully watching his breathing, ready to step in and end their game watching party if his pain became too intense.

Charity was also concerned for the little boy, picking up on the pain he was trying to hide from the two adults in the room. She knew he was hoping to prolong the party atmosphere that Maddie had helped create, but not telling them about his pain could have disastrous consequences later this evening.

Zach's face looked relieved at her offer of pain meds and Maddie immediately headed for the hallway. "I'll be back in a minute."

Nick shook his head at Zach and then helped him back to the hospital bed by picking him up and physically transferring him. "Buddy, I thought we talked about not ignoring your pain?"

"I didn't want this to end," Zach's face fell.

Nick picked up his fragile wrist and started mentally counting his heart rate. "Slow down your breathing, Zach. Everything's going to be fine."

Maddie returned with two syringes. She injected the first one into his IV and then adjusted the drip. "Here it comes, kiddo. Count backward from twenty and you should start to feel a whole lot better. Twenty. Nineteen."

Zach continued to count, "Eighteen. Seventeen. Sixteen. Fifteen. Fourteen. Thirteen."

Charity continued to count silently with Zach as Nick moved up beside Maddie.

"Nice technique," Nick whispered.

"If they're counting, they aren't holding their breath," she murmured back.

"Like I said, good idea. In fact, you've got so many good ideas, I'm thinking you need to start writing them down as sort of a cheat sheet for other nurses and CNAs."

Maddie shook her head as a blush crept into her cheeks. "I don't think so."

Nick nodded and then turned back to Zach and finished counting with him. "Three. Two. One."

"Better?" Maddie asked.

"Yeah."

"Good. Try to get some rest. Want me to stay until you fall asleep?" Nick asked.

Zach shook his head, even as his eyes closed, and he mumbled, "No."

Charity watched as Nick gave the little boy a tender look and then leaned over and kissed his forehead. "Goodnight, son. Sleep well."

Nick stood up and then looked at Maddie, becoming self-conscious and shifting from foot to foot. He cleared his throat and then nodded toward the door, "Let's talk outside."

Maddie nodded and preceded him from the room. Once the door was closed, Nick sighed and then smiled at her. "You are an amazing nurse and I can't thank you enough for what you did for Zach tonight."

Maddie shook her head. "I didn't do all that much. I brought him pizza and we watched a football game together."

"Yes, but that is more normal than he's had in months. You gave that to him and I'm forever grateful."

Charity watched Maddie nod her head once and then turn and walk away. Nick looked like he wanted to go after her. He even took a step in her direction, but his pager went off, so he pulled back to answer it.

Charity started to go after Maddie, but she was needed back in the heavenly realm. She filed tonight's activities away, along with Maddie's emotions. She took comfort in the knowledge that, while Maddie had been here at the hospital doing something as mundane as watching a football game, she hadn't been at the cemetery grieving Miah. It was only a small step, but a move in the right direction, nonetheless.

Chapter 10

The next day...

Maddie sat outside the cemetery early in the morning, desperately needing to resume her normal routine of visiting Miah's gravesite. She'd slept poorly the night before, dreams of both Miah and Dr. Nick that seemed to be all jumbled up and caused her to wake several times, disoriented and unsettled. Right after Miah's death, Maddie had suffered from terrible nightmares. In each one, Miah had been trying to get to her but died a horrible, gruesome death. These images would rip her from sleep and leave her screaming and crying out. When she would fully awaken and realize that he truly was dead, she would scream and cry even harder at the unfairness of it all.

Coming to the cemetery had been her way of dealing with her grief. These last five days without access to Miah's gravesite had taken a toll. Today, she had dark circles under her eyes and a monster migraine hovered, ready to strike. She was trying, very unsuccessfully, to stave it off. She was hoping that the few minutes she spent at the cemetery would help ground her a bit and allow her to continue pretending everything in her world was fine for one more day.

She remembered both her snow boots and her gloves this morning. She slid from the vehicle and gingerly trekked through the snow. Since the cemetery had been closed to visitors, none of the walks had been shoveled. For the last few days, several feet of snow had fallen over the city. Traversing it was exhausting.

She stopped when she was next to the guard shack, looking for the large pine tree that she always used as the landmark for where Miah's gravesite lay. She took a moment to pull her scarf tighter around her neck, shivering despite her warm clothing and winter gear. The wind was brutal today and it felt like it was blowing right through her winter coat.

She trudged on, her boots weighing her feet down more and more with each step. She finally stopped where she thought Miah's headstone lay nestled in the grass, but she couldn't be sure. "I need to put a bench or something out here so I can find it even in the dark without a flashlight." Her words were carried away on the wind, but that made them no less true. With the amount of accumulated snow on the ground, she was operating completely blind.

She used her gloves to dig down through the snow, her hands moving to and fro, as she attempted to locate the edge of the marble. She finally located something hard and worked her way around the edges, only to be disappointed when it turned out to be someone else's headstone.

Her fingers were freezing as her gloves were not meant to be digging in the snow and not waterproof in any way. They were now wet as well, and her shivering had increased tenfold. She stood up, feeling so lost as to what she should do, but no answers appeared in the form of a voice from the sky. To make matters worse, it started to snow, great big, wet flakes that stuck to her hair in no time.

She looked at the place where she thought Miah's headstone lay and was torn between wanting to see and touch it before she headed back to her car or risking her health by staying out here one moment longer. Another shiver determined her course of action and she headed back to her vehicle. She reached the car and sat there for long moments with the heater going full blast. She removed her wet gloves and it felt as if snow had gotten down into her boots but there was nothing she could do about it right this minute.

Disappointed that she'd not been able to talk to him, she leaned her head against the steering wheel, not caring that she was only moments from being late to work. Right now, she didn't care. She took several steadying breaths, but the unsettled feeling wouldn't go away. After several minutes and finally being able to feel her fingertips again, she put the car in reverse and pulled back out onto the road. A glance at the dashboard clock told her she was going to be at least ten minutes late.

She scrambled for her cellphone, hitting the speed dial button for the operator and hoping everyone on the third floor was calm this morning.

"St. Mary's, how may I direct your call?"

"Pediatrics."

"Hold, please."

Maddie pushed the speakerphone button and then moved the vehicle forward through the now, white road. She heard the hospital's elevator music come across the line, Christmas music that was both soothing and uplifting, but

Maddie didn't really hear it. This was the second Christmas she'd had to survive without Miah, and the harder of the two.

"Peds, this is Marci."

"Hey, Marci, this is Maddie."

"Maddie, we were just wondering if something had happened to you. Is everything okay?"

"I'm just running a bit late." Maddie felt the tires slip on a patch of ice and she tightened her hands on the steering wheel, trying to keep the vehicle going in the right direction, but her focus was split between driving and the phone call and the more she tried to correct the slide, the more out of control the vehicle became.

"Okay. I'll let everyone know."

"Thank...oh no!" Maddie panicked as the vehicle started sliding sideways, the front end no longer facing the road, but the side of the road where large trees and leafless bushes acted like a barrier to the land beyond.

"Maddie?"

"I...," she couldn't talk. It all happened so fast. One minute the vehicle was sliding on the icy road, the next she was sliding into a tree, the front tires becoming stuck in the deep ditch as the rear tires continued to spin, pushing the vehicle up and over onto its side and top. Maddie felt her seatbelt pull against her chest as she was rocked with the vehicle's movement.

"Maddie?"

Maddie heard Marci's voice coming from somewhere inside the vehicle, but she was struggling to catch her breath and not panic. She quickly took stock of any injuries, not coming up with any that seemed serious, just some bumps and bruises.

"Maddie? Girl, you'd better answer me. What's happening?"

"Marci..."

"Thank goodness. What happened? You were talking to me and then suddenly it sounded like you had an accident..."

"I did." Maddie tried to calm her breathing down as she tried to reach the keys in the ignition to turn the vehicle off. Any and all survival and trauma information came rushing at her and she knew she needed to turn the vehicle off and then see if she could get herself out of the vehicle. Just in case there was a fuel leak or a small fire getting ready to start.

"Marci…I…"

"Did you say you wrecked?" the CNA's voice came back at her.

"Yes."

"Where are you? I'll send help."

"By the cemetery," Maddie told her. Her head was beginning to hurt along with her neck and chest. Her fingertips finally came in contact with the key and she stretched as far as she could and managed to turn it backward, shutting off the engine of the vehicle.

Two things immediately made themselves known – it was going to get cold very quickly, and her other arm was pinned beneath her and the center console. She tried to shift her weight so that she could undo her seatbelt, but the car was tipped too far to the side and each movement put more pressure on her already screaming shoulder. It didn't feel dislocated, but it was being strained by her position to the point she knew she'd be sore for several days once she got free.

"Cemetery? What are you doing all the way out there? Sorry. Guess it doesn't matter. Do you need an ambulance? Can you get out of the vehicle? Are you injured?"

"Wait…," Maddie tried to get the CNA to calm down, but the initial adrenaline dump was wearing off and she suddenly felt so tired. She felt almost like she wasn't really in her body and she lifted her free hand to her head to try and rub some feeling back into it, only to encounter a sticky substance that upon visual inspection was blood.

Maddie had been a nurse for several years and the sight of blood wasn't one to normally panic her, but she was several miles from the epicenter of town, she couldn't get herself out of the vehicle, and now she was bleeding from her head. Those three things had complication written all over them.

She heard Marci talking to others she assumed were her co-workers and she closed her eyes as she tried to keep panic from taking away her ability to think logically. She counted her breaths, ignoring how cold it was beginning to get in the vehicle.

"Maddie?" Dr. Nick's voice came to her foggy mind.

"What?" she called out, forcing herself to open her eyes. "I'm in here. I'm stuck. Dr. Nick? Where are you?"

"I thought you said she wasn't injured?" his voice came from somewhere farther away.

"She said she wasn't hurt. Maddie, what's wrong?" Marci's voice held more urgency now.

"Marci it's okay. Dr. Nick's here," Maddie told her.

"What? She's not making any sense," another voice she didn't recognize floated into the vehicle.

"Where is she?" Dr. Nick asked.

"I'm right here," Maddie told him, her head beginning to throb now. "My head hurts. Can you get me out of here?"

"Hey, Maddie, can you answer a couple of questions for me?" his voice came back.

"Uh huh."

"Good girl. You said your head hurts, did you hit it?"

"I don't...I'm bleeding."

"From your head?"

"I guess so. My shoulder really hurts. Why can't you get me out of here? It's cold."

"Maddie, it's Teresa. The ambulance and fire personnel are headed your way, but the road conditions and multiple accidents are slowing them down. Hang in there."

Maddie giggled. "Not a problem since I can't reach my seatbelt. I don't know how monkeys do this without having a headache all the time."

"Monkeys?"

"Maybe the car tipped over?"

"I'm heading out there. I'm at least 10 minutes closer to her than the emergency vehicles headed her way."

"Dr. Nick it's your day off..."

"So, I can do with it whatever I please. Maddie, hang in there. Helps on the way."

"What about...?" Teresa's voice jumped into the conversation.

"Hi, Teresa. I'm going to be late to work," Maddie told her, finally getting to the reason she'd placed the call to begin with.

"Okay, hon. You just sit tight until help arrives, okay?"

Maddie nodded but then caught herself when pain increased everywhere. "Okay." She caught snippets of other conversations, something to do with Paula and donor list, but she couldn't make sense of any of it and didn't have the energy to ask.

"This is all your fault, Miah. All of it."

"Who's she talking to? Is there someone else in the car with her?" Nick's voice asked. "Maddie, who's in the car with you?"

"What?" she asked, confusion in her voice.

"We heard you talking to someone else. Miah? Is he hurt?"

"Can't hurt a dead person, doc. Didn't they teach you that in med school?" Maddie asked, her speech slightly slurred. Her head was really beginning to hurt now.

"Did she say someone was dead?" Marci's voice asked.

"Miah's dead," Maddie interjected, sorrow welling up inside her chest as she said the words aloud. Grief was like a sledgehammer, tearing apart the walls she'd carefully built over the last year by visiting his gravesite and pretending that somehow this was just an extension of his deployment. It wasn't logical, but Maddie hadn't been willing to face the concept that Miah and the life they'd dreamed of was never going to happen. He'd abandoned her.

Suddenly, she was angry. Furious and the need to scream and hit something grew inside of her. She wasn't mad at the military or the people who had placed the IED in the road that had taken Miah's life. She was mad at Miah. How dare he leave her here to go through life without him. He'd promised to come back to her. They were supposed to have been married right after New Year's. He had betrayed her by leaving. Uncontrollable emotions roared to life as tears streamed down her face.

She was mad at God, too. He'd allowed Miah to leave her. He could have kept him safe, but He didn't. He let him die over there in that desert. God had abandoned her as well.

"Maddie, shush. Dr. Nick's on his way. He should be there in about five minutes." Teresa, Marci and several other nameless voices continued to talk to her and to each other.

Maddie heard Teresa's calming voice, but it didn't matter. She needed to tell Miah how much she hated him for leaving her. To do that, she needed to go where he was. She would tell Miah how much he'd hurt her. Then, maybe she could move forward with her life.

Why does my head hurt? She frowned, sensing that there was something off with her thinking. *No! I just need to tell Miah and God that I'm mad at them.*

Chapter 11

Nick was trying not to panic, but Maddie had been in an accident. She was trapped in the vehicle and bleeding from her head. And she sounded very confused at the moment. He was unsure if there was another person in the vehicle with her, but as he carefully navigated the icy roads, he hoped she'd been talking about something that had happened in the past. His impression of Maddie was one of compassion and empathy. She would have a really hard time dealing with another person's death if she thought she'd had anything to do with it.

He reached the last intersection and was relieved to see both an ambulance and firetruck approaching from the opposite direction. He didn't wait for them, but turned left and headed toward the cemetery, keeping his eyes peeled for signs of Maddie's little red Civic.

There!

His heart skipped a beat when he saw the underside of Maddie's vehicle sticking up from the bank, the nose end of the vehicle not visible from this position. He carefully drove and parked just beyond her vehicle to leave room for the others. With gloves in hand, he exited his SUV and made his way toward Maddie's car.

"Maddie?" he called in through the shattered windshield. It was still held together by the safety coating. He used his gloves to brush away the accumulating snow, eyeing the sky and murmuring, "A little help about now, God, would be much appreciated."

He could see her, still hooked to her seat by the belt stretched tight across her chest. Her head was bleeding, but without getting inside to examine her, he didn't know if that was the cause of her confusion, or just a contributing factor.

The sound of sirens died out as the ambulance and firetruck arrived.

"What have we got?"

"Dr. Nick Stavros. Maddie's one of my nurses and she called in to say she was going to be late and wrecked while on the phone with one of the other girls on the floor. She's got a head laceration and was pretty confused as of ten minutes ago."

The firefighters swarmed the vehicle, taking stock of the situation before working to stabilize the vehicle and release Maddie from the seatbelt.

"What's her name?" one of the firefighters asked.

"Maddie."

The man nodded and then called in to her, "Maddie, we're going to try and get you out of there. The fastest way to do that is to remove this glass. Can you hear me?"

There was no response or movement from inside the vehicle. The leader nodded, giving the signal for them to hook the windshield glass and pull it away from the vehicle. Two of the men forced metal hooks into the top of the shattered glass and then in a coordinated move, they pulled back sharply, removing the entire windshield and rubber seal around the car.

Another firefighter quickly gained access to Maddie and called out, "She's unconscious. I need a C-collar and a backboard."

The items requested were produced. Several of the emergency personnel carefully transferred Maddie to the yellow board as the seatbelt was cut free. They removed her from the vehicle and transferred her to a gurney. Nick followed them as they started toward the ambulance.

"Is there anyone else in the car?" Nick asked.

The firefighter shook his head. "No, just her. Why?"

"Nothing, she seemed to be talking to someone else and I thought maybe she was talking to a passenger."

"No, she was the only one in the car which is very lucky. Anyone sitting in the passenger seat might have gotten seriously injured when it crashed and tipped this way."

"Good to know." Nick watched as they checked the vehicle for fuel leaks and then retrieved her purse and phone. "I'll take those."

He took them and then followed the gurney to the ambulance.

"Guys, I know this is your call, but I'm a doctor and she works for me. May I?"

The paramedics both nodded, "Go for it. We can only do so much without calling in for clearance anyway."

"Start an IV," Nick spoke quietly. He checked her pupils, disliking the fact that one of her eyes wasn't responding as fast as the other. "Possible concussion. Call ahead to the hospital and have them get her scheduled for a STAT CT so we know what we're dealing with."

"Hey, doc, you want one of us to drive your rig back to the hospital?" one of the firefighters asked.

"That would be helpful. Keys are still in it."

"Gotcha. See you up there." The firefighter closed the ambulance doors and, seconds later, they were moving with their sirens going.

Nick continued to assess her condition, talking softly to her, but she never opened her eyes the entire ride or appeared to regain consciousness. He put a light dressing on her head laceration, unwilling to clean or stitch while in a moving vehicle and definitely not until he knew for sure she didn't have a closed head injury.

He watched her, feelings for her building as they always did when she was around. He'd come to really like this young woman and he wasn't sure what it was about her that drew him toward her, like a moth to a flame, but it was there and wouldn't be denied. Nick had never fallen this quickly or this hard for another woman. He found it highly disconcerting to his peace of mind.

There was something between the two of them that bore further investigation and exploration, but first, he needed to make sure she was okay and ready for what came next. They'd figure out this chemistry between them along the way.

• • ✿ • •

CHARITY HOVERED IN the corner of the ambulance, watching as Nick tended to the unconscious Maddie. Charity had already sent up a request for information about Maddie's future and been assured that she was in no danger of dying at this time. While that was a relief to Charity, she wasn't going to take any chances that this event might undo whatever progress Maddie had made in the last few days.

Nothing happened without a reason, even though that reason might never be revealed to those involved. Charity had to believe that this was all part of the greater plan.

"Problems, little angel?" Matthias' voice came from her left.

Charity turned and saw her mentor hovering nearby. "I didn't know you came down to Earth."

"I don't do so very often, but I truly want to see you succeed in helping Maddie move on with her life."

"The accident..." she began, but Matthias lifted a hand and cut her off.

"Is designed to be a wake-up call for young Maddie. It's time she faces reality."

"I agree. This might be the incident that makes her start to question how she's been handling her fiancé's death."

"Yes, but this could also force her to withdraw once again."

There had to be a reason for this accident, Charity just needed to be prepared to help Maddie take advantage of whatever it was when it was revealed.

Matthias gave her an encouraging smile. "Your job is to make sure she only moves forward. I have faith in you." He disappeared just as quickly as he'd appeared, leaving Charity to hover in the corner of the ambulance as it completed its trek across town to the hospital. She sent prayers into the heavens, having every confidence that, since nothing happened by chance, this was all part of God's overall plan for Maddie's future. Charity simply got to be a part of making it all happen.

She turned her attention to Nick and the obvious concern and worry coming off of him in waves. She'd been thrilled with the attraction Nick and Maddie had shown for one another, albeit Nick wasn't her charge, but there was absolutely no reason she couldn't include him in her guardian duties.

Nick was one of those people whose compassion and empathy for others made him an excellent physician and a great human being. But where others might stop with merely understanding another's pain, Nick had a driving need to fix whatever was wrong. Charity was sure that, once Maddie started down the road to recovery, Nick would try to fix whatever was wrong in her life as well.

Charity could use that to her advantage. Where she couldn't communicate directly with her human charges – only archangels had that ability – at least she could encourage others to do so. Little hints, clues that brought back memories of days past, could push someone in a direction they might have been considering but not fully committed to. The trick was doing so without breaking any of the Angel Codes.

Angels were not allowed to influence human emotions. They weren't allowed to make two people feel love where it didn't exist. They weren't allowed to skew feelings about a past event, if those feelings didn't truly exist. That wasn't to say that they couldn't do those things. They simply were against the rules.

With this being Charity's third and final challenge, she wasn't about to jeopardize her graduation by violating the rules now. No, she just needed to provide opportunities for Maddie to exercise her free will and acknowledge her feelings, her needs, and her wants. The same was true for Nick, but Charity was hoping that some of his feelings, needs, and wants would align with Maddie's.

It was time for Maddie to move on with her life, after suffering such a great loss, and to deal with the past. She hadn't been able to do that on her own, but she'd already acknowledged that she needed to do just that. Charity intended to make sure she stayed the course and followed through on those last thoughts. A bright new life full of sunshine and happiness awaited Maddie on the other side of her grief. It would hurt crossing that bridge, but it must be done. And Charity would be by her side the entire way, leading her and giving her strength and courage as it was needed.

Chapter 12

"Doctor, we're pulling into the hospital now," the paramedic driving the ambulance called back.

Nick nodded and then picked up Maddie's wrist once more. "Her pulse is holding steady."

The ambulance stopped and the back doors opened. A team of doctors and nurses from the hospital were right there to offer their assistance. Nick stepped off the ambulance and immediately drew curious looks from the ER nurses.

"Dr. Stavros?"

Nick ignored the question in their looks and voices and instead addressed Dr. Peters, the lead doctor in the emergency department. "Kevin, she has a head laceration. They called ahead to reserve a CT scan of her head."

Kevin Peters nodded. "They're ready for her as soon as we can make sure she's stable."

Nick held onto his impatience, knowing the ER had protocols in place for the protection of both the patients and the medical personnel. "Do what you need to do."

Nick did his best to stay out of everyone's way, which was made more difficult because the doctors and nurses kept looking to him for confirmation that they were doing the right thing. He finally took himself off to the third floor to make sure the "elves" knew Maddie was at the hospital and getting checked out.

He stepped out of the elevator and instantly he had nurses, CNAs, parents, and patients clamoring for news of Maddie. She was the newcomer to the third-floor family, but she had quickly proven herself an excellent nurse and good listener. Both things desperately needed on a hospital ward where the majority of patients were under the age of twelve and dealing with life-threatening illnesses like cancer and organ failure.

"How is she?"

"Is she still confused?"

Nick held up his hand before another question could be fired at him and, in a quiet and very calm voice, informed them that she was unconscious. She did have a small cut on her head that would require stitches, but first she was getting a CT scan. He told them that he would be back with more news as soon as possible.

"Give her our best when she wakes up," Marci told him, as he turned and headed for the stairs.

Nick nodded. "I will."

Teresa waited until the parents and patients had dispersed and then she motioned him to the side. "Sarah's been moved up to the first place on the transplant list. I took the liberty of telling her mom and aunt the good news. I hope you don't mind?"

"Not at all," Nick assured her.

Teresa nodded and then lowered her voice and asked somberly. "What do you want to do about Paula?"

Nick sighed and felt a measure of guilt that he'd not been able to meet with her parents this morning. It was his day off, but he'd come into the hospital for the express purpose of helping them make some tough decisions about how the young girl was going to spend her last days. He'd honestly been expecting a phone call for the last twenty-four hours saying that she had passed away, but instead, she seemed to have rallied once more.

"She's still stable?" he asked, taking the tablet Teresa produced and reviewing her vitals over the last few days. "She's getting stronger. She's not asking for pain meds?"

"No, in fact, when I tried to give them to her this morning, she said she wasn't hurting and didn't want them. Her mother and I convinced her to take a half dose, just in case she started hurting again. We need to keep ahead of the pain."

"I agree and you did the right thing. Let me go look in on her before I head down to radiology. Who's with her right now?"

"Her parents and her brother."

"Okay." Nick headed down the hallway, saying a silent prayer for wisdom in this situation. He stepped into the room and smiled at the sound of Paula's weak laughter. It was one of the best things about the little girl. It wrenched at

Nick's soul that he couldn't find a cure for her cancer. This was the part of his job that just flat sucked – plain and simple.

"Hey, guys. How's my best patient doing this morning?"

"Hi, Dr. Nick. I feel good today," Paula told him.

"That's good to hear." Her parents gave him questioning looks and he went through the motions of checking her vitals and then nodding. "How's the pain level?"

"I didn't have to take a full dose this morning..."

"That's good as well. Tommy how are you doing?" he asked her brother who was immersed in a handheld gaming device.

Tommy looked up and nodded. "I'm okay. Does Paula get to come home for Christmas?"

Nick glanced at both parents and then tipped his head toward the doorway. "I tell you what, why don't you keep your sister company and we'll go discuss that."

He led the way into the hallway and then addressed the matter head on. "Is that what you are wanting to do? Take her home for Christmas?"

They shared a sad look and then nodded. "We'd like to, but what if she starts hurting again? What will we..."

"I can give you some oral Morphine to take home with you. It works amazingly fast and all you have to do is place it under her tongue. That would give her some relief while she's transported back here."

They looked at one another and then Paula's dad nodded. "Then that's what we'll do." It was obvious that the man was having a hard time containing his emotions, but he continued, "She almost begged us to take her home so that she could sit by the Christmas tree. I didn't have the heart to tell her that we didn't get a tree this year."

His wife wrapped her arms around him. Nick found himself struggling to contain his own emotions. Unless a miracle happened, Paula would be lucky to make it through this Christmas, let alone one a year and some days from now.

"Folks, I know this is hard. I can't even imagine how hard, but I have no problem setting things in motion for you to take Paula home and let her spend some quality time with her family. I won't sugarcoat it for you, you know that, but she most likely doesn't have much time.

"If you want to take her home, I'll speak with the nurses and have them arrange a hospice nurse to come and stay with you for as long as necessary."

They gave him grateful looks and, when Brian folded his wife into his arms, Nick silently made his way back down to the nurse's station. Teresa was waiting for him. He told her, "Call Laurie and have her arrange for one of her hospice nurses to come up here and meet Paula's parents and then make arrangements for them to take her home as soon as possible." He scribbled a couple of prescriptions down and then handed them to the nurse. "See that the pharmacy downstairs fills these and give the hospice nurse my personal cell phone number when she arrives. I'd like routine updates on Paula's condition for the duration of her stay at home."

"Is she..." Teresa asked, unable to finish the question.

Nick nodded once. "Say your farewells. I doubt you'll get another chance."

Teresa's eyes filled with tears and she turned away, as Nick did the same. Working on this floor had many perks, but it also came with devastating news and the impending death of one of their long-term patients always gutted the nurses and doctors involved in their care. Nick rubbed a hand over his neck as Paula's dad's words came rushing back. He cleared his throat. "Do you still have the number of those folks that came up to visit Paula a few weeks back? The neighbors and such?"

Teresa nodded and pulled a yellow sticky note from the back of the file. "One of the men gave me his number and told me to call if we thought of anything they could do for either Paula or her parents."

Nick nodded and met Teresa's eyes. "Call him and tell him they are bringing Paula home for Christmas. She's expecting to celebrate with her family like always, with a tree and decorations, but they didn't put one up this year."

Teresa nodded her understanding and reached for the phone. "Enough said. I'll make sure everything's taken care of, even if a few of us have to go over and help. It'll be a few hours before they get to leave here...that should be plenty of time."

Nick smiled and then included the others who were standing nearby. "That includes all of you. Thank you."

The women gathered around nodded. He spied the clock hanging on the wall and his focus shifted. "I need to go check on Maddie."

"I'll take care of things here for Paula."

"Thank you." Nick quickly wiped his tears away, then headed for the elevator. He spoke to a few parents on the way, all inquiring about Maddie's condition. She'd become a part of the team with ease and everyone liked her. Everyone. As the elevator headed down to the main floor, he acknowledged that he was no different. He liked her a little too much for a working relationship, but he wasn't so concerned with keeping to his rules about fraternization where she was concerned. There was something about her that he couldn't ignore. It commanded his attention and begged for further research into what it might mean for his future. For both of their futures.

Chapter 13

The elevator dinged and Nick stepped off, turned to his left and then headed down to the radiology department. Maddie was currently in the CT scanner. He stood behind the control desk with the radiologist as the images began to appear on the screens. Nick scanned them with a critical eye, growing more and more relieved as the minutes passed.

"Looks good," the radiologist, Mike Fullman, told Nick as they finished the scan. "I'll take a closer look, but right now I don't see anything of interest."

Nick nodded. "Thanks."

She was loaded back onto the transfer gurney. Nick escorted the orderly and her back down to the emergency department. He sat in the exam room with her, checking his email and texting the third floor to let them know she was doing okay. He was just about to head back upstairs to check on Paula and her family, but Maddie took that moment to wake up.

"Nick?"

He spun around and smiled at her. "There you are. You decided to take a nice long nap. How are you feeling?"

"My head still hurts," she told him. She looked around the room and then frowned. "Why am I in the emergency room?"

He was much relieved upon hearing her identify her current location. "Don't you remember what happened?" Nick asked her.

Maddie blinked several times and then lifted a hand up to her head, gingerly felt the bandage there, and then she groaned. "I slid on the ice."

"Yeah. You put your car in the ditch," Nick told her.

He was standing over her bedside now, and he pulled the penlight from his pocket and shined it into each of her eyes before asking her to follow his finger. Her pupils appeared more normal now, but she was tracking a little slow for his comfort level. He pocketed the penlight and then told her, "You hit your head and you've got a slight concussion."

"I concur, one hundred percent," Dr. Peters said as he entered the room behind them. He handed over the chart for Nick to quickly scan the official radiologist's report before handing it back.

"So, she going home?" Nick asked.

"As long as she has someone with her for the next twenty-four to thirty-six hours, that should be fine."

Nick saw Maddie's mouth drop open and he cut her off. "I'll have one of the girls from three bring her down an extra set of scrubs to put on."

"Just a minute," Dr. Peters asked. He turned to Maddie and asked, "Do you have someone at home you want the nurse to call for you?"

Maddie shook her head. "I live alone."

"Is there someone you can call to come and stay with you?"

Maddie started to shake her head but ended up only making her head throb and herself nauseous. Holding very still she whispered with as much conviction as she could muster, "I'll be okay. I'm a nurse."

"She's coming home with me," Nick stated, meeting Maddie's shocked stare.

"No, I..."

"Wonderful. Today is your day off?" Dr. Peters asked.

"Yes, I just came by to...." His words were cut off when his pager went off. He glanced at it and then frowned. "I need to make a quick call. I'll be right back."

He stepped outside the cubicle, picked up the nearest hallway phone, and dialed the third floor.

"Pediatrics, this is Teresa. Can I help you?"

"Teresa, this is Dr. Nick. You paged me?"

"Yes, it's Zach."

"What happened?" Nick asked trying to keep the panic from his voice.

"He heard that Maddie was in an accident, and he lost it. He won't quit crying and no matter how many of us have assured him she's going to be alright; he won't settle down. I don't think he's going to calm down until he sees her for himself."

Nick nodded and then told Teresa, "Tell Zach that I'll bring Maddie up in just a few minutes."

"Is that wise?" Teresa asked.

"I can't have him upset. It's not good for him. Maddie's being sent home with me for a minor concussion. I'll being her up before I take her home."

"To your home?" Teresa questioned.

"Yes. I'll let you know in the morning whether she'll be working at all or just part of her shift tomorrow."

"I already let Penny and Ciera know what was going on, and Penny offered to come in tomorrow as well. She's supposed to be on four days' vacation, but she came in anyway."

"Thank her for me."

"She's already here. You can probably do that in person when you come up. I also contacted Dr. Sherman, and he is prepared to cover tomorrow for you as well."

That was unexpected news, and where Nick lived to make his patients' lives better, the thought of having to leave Maddie as soon as tomorrow morning wasn't at all pleasant. "Please thank him for me and let him know I accept and will make it up to him at some point in the future."

"I'll do that. Paula's going home in a few hours, her house is being taken care of by neighbors, and the hospice nurse is due to arrive before the end of the hour," Teresa caught him up.

"You've been busy."

"Just spreading a little Christmas cheer where we can. See you in a few minutes?"

"Yes. Tell Zach I'm going to bring Maddie up in the next half hour."

"Will do. Is she truly alright?"

"She is, or she will be. She has a killer headache and is pretty tired emotionally, but she has nothing to do but rest and sleep for the next few days."

"Good, she always looks exhausted. I'm not sure she sleeps well at night, even without having an accident."

"Let's see if we can't work on that."

"Will do. See you in a bit," Teresa disconnected the call. Nick went back inside the cubicle to see the doctor going over Maddie's discharge instructions.

"I was just telling Maddie that she needed to put aside the brave face and communicate if her headache worsened, she became dizzy, or felt out of control."

"I'm not going anywhere, so I'll keep an eye on her. I see someone brought the scrubs down for her."

"I actually sent one of the interns up to retrieve them. I figured they were probably already operating shorthanded."

"They're actually doing just fine. They called in the nurse who was on vacation and she agreed to help out for as long as needed."

"Good. You've got a crew up there most of us would kill for," Dr. Peters told him. "I can't find enough people down here to fill the normal shifts, let alone want to pick up extra hours."

"Working on the third floor is like nothing else. I only keep the best and those that have proven themselves to be capable of fitting into the culture I've created up there."

Dr. Peters laughed, "I've heard about your culture. Makes the rest of our jobs seem boring."

Nick chuckled, having heard that same comment from other doctors. "Feel free to borrow my motto - Work is fun and fun creates a healing environment."

Dr. Peters scoffed, "Try telling that to an overdosed teenager who is furious we're pumping his stomach. Lots of fun kids."

"You know what I was getting at," Nick told him with a roll of his eyes.

Kevin nodded. "I'm just giving you a bad time. I understand completely, but fun and the emergency room don't mix well together."

"I know that. Let me round up a wheelchair and then I'll get her out of here."

"I can have one of the nurses meet you at the discharge ramp, if you like?" Dr. Peters offered.

"Actually, we have to make a quick trip up to the third floor before she can get out of here. There's a little boy upstairs who heard about her accident and is convinced she's dying."

"Zach?" Maddie asked, finally joining in on the conversation.

Nick nodded. "He's pretty upset, and Teresa asked if you could pop into his room and assure him you're going to be fine before I take you home."

"Of course. He's lost so much...he must be terrified. We should go now," she looked up at him with big eyes filled with the remnants of her headache and empathy for the little boy that had stolen his heart. He was afraid this woman could easily steal his heart as well. In fact, he was already more than halfway there.

Nick brought his attention back to the room and met Dr. Peters' frown. "We won't stay but a minute, but Zach needs to see her. They've bonded at a deeper level than anyone else up on the third floor."

"Can't his parents…"

"He's orphaned, at least until he gets discharged. Then…well, then we'll see." He turned to face Maddie, only to see that she'd done a credible job of sitting up on the side of the bed, without jerking her IV out of her arm, and was searching for the bed control so that she could lower it down and get out.

"Where do you think you're going?"

"Upstairs. You said…"

"I'd round up a wheelchair and then we'd go upstairs. You're not walking anywhere inside the hospital today," Nick informed her.

"But…"

Nick arched a brow at her and watched her shoulders sag. "Fine. But can we go now?"

Dr. Peters handed Nick her discharge instructions and then whispered, "Good luck. Nurses make horrible patients."

Nick nodded his head and then thanked the nurse who entered with a wheelchair. "Your chariot has arrived."

Maddie eyed the chair distastefully and groused about having to use it. "You know it's hospital policy."

"For patients…"

"Which you were as of an hour ago. Relax and enjoy the ride."

Nick pushed her to the elevator and a few minutes later they were disembarking on the third floor in the midst of worried co-workers, patients, and parents. He watched as she tried to act normal and dispel everyone's worries about her health, but he'd seen her downstairs and was almost certain she had a pounding headache.

As he watched her push aside her own needs, he was struck with admiration for her strength. She had drawn his eye the first time he'd met her, and each interaction since then had only solidified his need to know more about her. He'd been fighting the attraction he felt toward her, telling himself that he would be crossing a line that, while not necessarily wrong, would probably be unwise. Nick had never before been tempted to mix his professional life with his personal life. Until now. Until Maddie walked into his life.

Chapter 14

The Heavenly Realms...

Charity was supposed to have met Hope at the cathedral fountains, but she'd waited an extra fifteen minutes, and she still hadn't shown. She headed for choir practice, and that's when she saw movement inside the schoolroom. She headed across the lawn and then paused in the doorway.

Hope was talking with Matthias and she didn't want to interrupt if they weren't finished. Matthias saw her and said something to Hope. When Hope turned toward her, Charity waved to her.

"Thank you, Matthias," Hope told the head of the guardian angel school before joining Charity outside. "Hi. What's up?"

"It's Joy. She's not feeling very joyful right now," Charity told her.

"Where is she?" Hope looked around the courtyard for her, but it was empty save for her and Charity.

"Down on Earth."

Hope smiled, "Let's go cheer her up."

Charity smiled back and with a nod, they were off. On their way, Charity explained what she knew of Joy's problem and Hope came up with several ideas of how to help her.

Several minutes later, they found Joy sitting in a bank of dirty snow, her face a study in what being forlorn must look like.

"Joy," Hope called her name softly as she and Charity came to a position on either side of her.

Joy turned, appearing shocked. "Hi! What are you two doing here?"

Hope shared a look with Charity and then explained, "We sensed that you were feeling a little lost. Is everything okay?"

"I thought so, but now..."

"Joy, you're not thinking of doing anything...illegal, are you?" Charity asked. As the most mature of the three, she often felt the need to adopt a motherly tone. Hope shook her head, giving silent support to Charity's warning.

"No! Believe me, I learned my lesson last year." Joy had caused quite a stir when she'd dared to interfere with human emotions and Matthias had been forced to step in and fix things.

Hope put an arm around Joy's shoulders. "We are all trying to do our very best. Have you talked to Matthias about whatever's not working?" Having just come from doing that exact thing, Hope knew their mentor was not only capable, but he'd just proven how willing he was to lend a helping hand.

"Not yet."

"Maybe you should go do that instead of sitting here moping around. It's the Christmas Season and no one, especially angels, should be moping in a pile of dirty, melted ice," Charity told her.

Joy looked down, and when she saw how dirty her gown had become, she gave both Hope and Charity a sheepish look. "Guess I should probably get cleaned up before I go see Matthias, huh?"

"I would strongly suggest that," Charity informed her with a smile.

Joy stood up and then gave the other two angels a confident nod. "I will figure this out. I just need to re-work my plan."

"With Matthias' help, right?" Hope inquired.

"Of course." Joy bid the other two angels farewell and then headed off.

Hope shared a smile with Charity. "Well, we did what we could. How are things going with your charge?"

Charity smiled, "Things are finally beginning to look up. It was touch and go there for a while. Today marks seven days where she hasn't spent most of her free time at the cemetery. I was beginning to think she was going to set down roots and become a permanent fixture there."

"Grief does such strange things to humans, even when they know where their loved ones have gone," Hope added.

"Yes. That being said, I should really go check on her. Matthias told me there was a miracle coming but refused to tell me in what respect. He said it was better if I didn't know because then I would be tempted to break the rules and he couldn't have that. Not on his watch."

"Miracles seem to be plentiful this time of year. One of my charges experienced a wonderful miracle today."

"One of your charges?" Charity asked. "I thought angels in training weren't allowed to have multiple charges?"

"We're not, but Matthias is bending the rules just a bit because my charges have a connection and while I was skeptical, they seem to be helping one another overcome the events of the past that have been keeping them from moving forward and living fulfilled and happy lives."

"Good luck. I'll see you at choir practice?" Charity asked as she and Hope headed up into the air. Chicago was a long way from Denver by human standards, but for an angel, it was nothing. Hope would be there before Claire took her next breath.

"Choir practice it is." Hope waved and, in an instant, she was gone. There was less than a week until Christmas. This year, Hope wanted Claire to spend it with people who knew how to laugh and enjoy life. She'd forgotten how to do both over the last four years.

Charity's charge needed to remember how to laugh, love, and enjoy life once again. Maddie had lost a lot a year ago, and somehow, Charity needed to make her remember that she was still alive. There was no honoring the life of a person lost when those left behind refused to move on with their lives. Now, if she could just keep Maddie moving in the right direction and prove to her that her life hadn't ended with Miah's death. If anyone needed a Christmas miracle, it was Maddie. And Charity intended to see that she was given every opportunity to heal.

• • ❧ • •

NICK PUSHED MADDIE toward Zach's room, having already gotten word that he wasn't calming down on his own. They arrived at his room and found him lying in his bed, tear stains on his cheeks as both Teresa and Marci tried to console him. When he saw Maddie sitting in the wheelchair, he sat up and then burst into a fresh bout of tears.

"Maddie!"

She looked up at Nick and he stopped their forward momentum and leaned down at her hand gesture. "What is it?"

"Stop and let me walk on my own. He's upset..."

"And you have a mild concussion and almost fell over when you stood up a few minutes ago to transfer from the bed to the chair," he reminded her with a frown.

She nodded once and then winced. "I know, but he needs to see that I'm okay. Please?"

It went against his better judgment, but he believed she was correct. He engaged the chair's brakes before stepping around to her side and giving her his arm to hold onto. She stood up and gripped his arm with both hands. He controlled the urge to wrap his arm around her and to find a way to erase the pain still lingering in her eyes. She'd received a few stitches to close the head laceration after the CT scan results had assured him that she didn't have a closed head injury. She was going to have quite a few bumps and bruises by morning. Considering what could have happened, her guardian angel was surely looking after her.

"Easy," he whispered, as she took her first step toward the bed and weaved slightly. He tightened his arm, holding one of her hands captive against his side.

"I'm okay," she whispered back.

"I'm not buying that, but hopefully Zach will."

He walked her over to the bedside and Teresa and Marci both excused themselves. Maddie released his arm and then sank down onto the side of the bed, unprepared when Zach threw himself into her arms and sobbed against her chest.

"I thought you were going to die. I don't want you to die," he sobbed.

"Shush. Hey, buddy. I just got a little bump on my head...oh, and my car's going to need some help, but I'm here and I'm okay."

"That's right, Zach. Maddie's going to be just fine. I promise."

Zach looked up at him, and Nick's heart broke at the look of desolation in his eyes. "Everyone dies."

"That's not true," Nick told him, going to sit on the other side of him. "Buddy, I know it seems that way, but it's just not true. Maddie didn't die..."

"My daddy did. And grandma left..."

Maddie made a pained sound, and he looked up to see her turning away so that Zach wouldn't see the tears streaming down her face. His heart went out to her, knowing she was feeling overly emotional. The connection she had with

Zach made her feel his pain in a way that others couldn't. He reached out and placed a comforting hand on her shoulder, then gave it a gentle squeeze.

She gave him a teary smile before turning back to Zach with a forced smile. "Hey, you know your grandma only went back to her home because she wasn't feeling very well, right? She was having some trouble remembering things and being back in her own home helps."

Zach was quiet for a minute and then whispered, "Do I have to go back there when I leave here?"

Maddie looked up at Nick, and he bit his lip before he tackled that loaded question. He had plans but hadn't really discussed them with Zach yet, not wanting to give the boy false hope of being cured or of the courts siding with Nick where custody of Zach was concerned. Nick turned so that he was looking directly at Zach and chose his words carefully.

"You know, we haven't really discussed what's going to happen once you're well enough to leave the hospital. That day is fast approaching. Maybe you should tell me what you want to happen?"

Zach chewed on his bottom lip for a moment. Nick was curious to hear the little boy's answer. If he wanted to go back and live with his grandmother and be near his aunts, uncles, and cousins, Nick would have to really think about what was best for Zach. That was what was most important, even though sending Zach away would break Nick's heart.

"Could I...," he paused.

"Could you what?" Nick asked quietly.

"Could I stay with you? I wouldn't be any trouble. I promise. I'd be real quiet and I don't eat very much..."

Maddie made another sound. Nick needed to handle this so he could get her home and put her to bed. "Zach, I would like nothing better than for you to stay here with me."

Zach's eyes lit up. He turned and grabbed hold of Maddie's hand. "Don't cry, Maddie. It'll be okay. Dr. Nick will make it all better, and I'll get to stay here. You and I can watch movies together and eat popcorn."

With a teary smile, Maddie nodded. "That sounds like a good plan, but you need to get better first. Did you take a nap today?"

Zach shook his head, hiding a yawn behind his hands. "I was too worried about you."

Maddie reached out and hugged him close. "I'm going to be okay, but I think we both need a nap."

She released Zach and his face brightened. "I know! You can take a nap here..."

"While that's a nice idea," Nick said, stepping in right away, "it just wouldn't work. Maddie needs to rest, but she can't go to sleep for a while yet because she hit her head really hard. I need to make sure she doesn't forget who she is."

Zach's eyes got great big as he asked, "She might forget who she is?"

Nick nodded solemnly. "It's been known to happen."

Zach gave Maddie a concerned look and then whispered loudly to Nick, "You make sure to tell her who she is, okay? Maybe you could make her a sign or something that she can look at. I don't want her to forget who I am."

"There's no chance of that happening." Nick was saved from having to continue the conversation when Teresa walked back in the room with a round of pain medicine and a lunch tray.

"Zach, since you didn't eat your breakfast, I thought you might want lunch early. They're going to be showing *How the Grinch Stole Christmas* in the common room right after lunch. I thought maybe you'd come watch it with me?"

"That's my favorite movie," Zach told the room.

"You say every movie is your favorite." Teresa smiled and then looked at Nick and Maddie. "You need to get her somewhere so she can rest." She eyed Maddie's face. "I realize gray is one of the new fashion colors this year, but it really doesn't do anything for Maddie's complexion."

Nick chuckled and looked at Maddie who was very pale and ashen. "I agree. Home it is. Zach, enjoy your movie and I'll see you tomorrow."

"And Maddie? Will she see me tomorrow?"

"We'll see how she feels in the morning." Nick wasn't going to commit her to doing anything just yet. While he was confident that she only had a slight concussion, he'd seen minor head injuries turn into week-long recoveries when people tried to do too much too soon. That would not be happening on his watch. "If she's not up to coming to visit, maybe she can talk to you on the phone for a bit. Either way, I'll be in to see you tomorrow, okay?"

Zachary nodded and then whispered loudly, "Make sure she doesn't forget who she is. She's my new friend, and I don't want her to forget me."

"I'll make sure," Nick promised. "Eat some lunch and rest so that you can enjoy your movie." He took Maddie's arm and led her back over to the wheelchair. "Let's get you home." He was silent as he wheeled her back to the elevator and then out to where his car had been parked by a very helpful firefighter.

Chapter 15

An hour later...

By the time Nick pulled into his garage, Maddie's head was hurting something fierce. She wanted to close her eyes and go to sleep. Each time her eyelids closed; Nick woke her up to force her to stay awake.

"Let's get you inside and settled in," he told her quietly. He came around and helped her out of the car, keeping one arm around her. They entered a very modern looking house with high ceilings and neutral colors on the walls and floors. Maddie tried to take in everything, but her head was pounding in time with her heartbeat. She just wanted to lie down and close her eyes for a few minutes.

Nick led her to a big, overstuffed couch, where she sank down. After removing her shoes, he swung her legs up on to the couch and pulled a fluffy blanket from a basket on the floor to drape over her. He tipped her chin up, took in her pale complexion and half-lidded eyes, and made a tsking sound.

"Head hurt?" he asked.

"Define hurt," she mumbled, letting her eyes close all the way.

"Poor baby."

Nick sat down on the couch, and she scooted over to make room for him. As she rolled toward him, she pressed her hips and back into the cushions on the couch. His hands smoothed her hair back off her face, and he gingerly skimmed his hand beneath her hair to gently rub her neck. "You can't have any painkillers for a few more hours. I know you want to go to sleep, but that's not going to happen, either."

Maddie moaned softly. His hands slowly pressing against the tight muscles in her neck eased the pain slightly. It was only early afternoon, and yet it felt like this day had been a series of days all run together. The emotional upheaval of the cemetery. The accident. Zachary. Nick being so kind to her.

Her head began to pound harder, and she moaned again, this time in obvious distress.

"Hey," Nick murmured softly to her. "You just got all tense. What's going through that brain of yours?"

"So many things," she murmured.

Nick leaned closer to her and then whispered, "Let them all go for today. Your brain needs to rest."

"I know, I just..."

Nick squeezed her shoulders and asked, "What's bothering you most?"

She took a moment before answering. "How safe I feel right now."

"Why does that worry you?" he asked.

"Because we don't really know one another. Yet, here I am...lying on your couch."

Nick stopped massaging her shoulders and withdrew his hands. He moved to sit on the coffee table, his hands dropping to rest between his knees. "You said you feel safe here."

"I do. That's the problem. I don't do this sort of thing."

"What sort of thing? Accept help from friends?"

"Are we friends? We don't really know much about one another."

"So, we'll change that. As for whether or not we are friends, I would like to believe we are. I like you, Maddie. And, to be completely honest, a bit more than I probably should. Do you not feel any sort of pull between us?"

Maddie's eyes meet his. "I don't want to."

Nick gave her a small smile. "Fair enough. I plan to find out why but not today or even tonight. Please know that right now, you are here because you needed help and that's what friends do. I want to be your friend. That's all for now. Can you let your worries go and let your body heal?"

"I can try," she finally murmured, dropping her eyes as a fresh stab of pain pushed through her brain.

"You're hurting. Lie down and try to relax."

Maddie didn't even try to nod. She lowered herself down to the couch, exhaling slowly to follow his directions. Slow, measured breaths had to relax the muscles in her neck and shoulders.

She slid her hands up and beneath the side of her head, releasing a sigh and willing the drum corps in her head to give it a rest. She silently vowed to be much more compassionate with her patients when they said their heads were killing them. She just wanted to close her eyes and let the world slip away. Along with it, the worries and sadness that kept trying to take over her thoughts.

"Hungry?" Nick asked softly.

Maddie shrugged one shoulder, "Not really, but it might help me stay awake."

"That's what I wanted to hear. How about grilled cheese and tomato soup?"

"With the squishy cheese?" she asked hopefully. In Maddie's opinion, that was the only way to make a grilled cheese sandwich. The processed cheese product melted easily and, when you cut the sandwich apart, it just kind of oozed out between the slices of bread.

"There is no other way," he gave her a smile and then stood up. "I'll bring you some tea as well."

"Thank you," she murmured, watching him head toward what she assumed was the kitchen. She forced herself to keep her eyes open, but she couldn't turn off her mind. She had wrecked because of the icy road conditions and the fact that her mind had been on God and Miah. Her anger came rushing back to the surface. A few seconds later, she pushed herself to a sitting position. She couldn't stay still with so many emotions moving through her body.

She suddenly needed to vent. Even with her head pounding like a jackhammer inside her skull, she felt an overwhelming need to scream and hit something. She clenched her fists after discovering that clenching her jaw sent unbelievable pain shooting through her skull. She sat on the couch, her nails digging crescent indentations in her palms, tears streaming down her face as she silently railed at Miah and God.

Why?! Why did You take him from me? We had our lives all planned out, and You took everything from me. I was always told You loved me, but this doesn't feel like love. I've spent the last year trying to pretend this was all a bad dream, but it's not. Miah isn't ever coming back. Ever!

"Maddie?" Nick's soft voice called to her from across the room. "Are you in pain?"

Maddie lifted sorrow-filled eyes to him and opened her mouth to speak, but the only thing that came out was a mournful cry. She tried to get ahold of herself, seeing the worry on his face, but she was so filled with anger and hurt, she couldn't even put it into words.

Nick seemed to understand. He came to her side, sat on the couch, and drew her into his arms. He whispered words of comfort as one hand stroked up and down her back in a slow motion. Rocking her slightly, he let her sob against his chest. Her hands fisted in his shirt as all of the grief and sadness of a love lost poured from her in a cathartic cleansing that was months overdue.

He never told her she needed to stop crying or that whatever was wrong was going to be okay. He simply held her, providing her a solid anchor and a friendly shoulder to cry on. A long time later, all cried out, Maddie lay against his chest. Her strength was completely gone now that she'd ripped the bandage off and lanced the festering wound in her soul.

Nick had settled back against the couch at some point during her crying frenzy and now she lay in his arms, his hand still stroking up and down her back in a soothing, monotonous motion. He leaned to the side and snagged a tissue box, pulling several free and pressing them into her hands.

Maddie wiped her face and then shivered as the remnant of a sob broke free.

"Better now?" Nick finally asked.

Maddie shrugged one shoulder. "I don't know."

"Want to talk about it?"

No. I never want to talk about it which is why I'm the way I am. "It's not something I talk about."

"It wasn't something you used to talk about," Nick corrected her. "Seems to me that, whatever it is, it needs to be shared. I'm here and not going any place."

When Maddie didn't offer any comment, Nick started trying to guess. "Does this have to do with your visit to the cemetery this morning?"

Maddie stiffened and then nodded once but didn't offer up any other information. She didn't want to discuss the cemetery or her frequent trips to visit Miah's grave.

"You said something while on the phone with us earlier...something about someone dying? Miah?"

Maddie felt exposed, the wound on her soul so raw. She wrapped her arms around herself, squeezing tightly in hopes she wouldn't fall apart again. She kept her eyes down and then whispered, "Jeremiah Shaw. He was a soldier."

"Ah. Killed in action?" Nick asked quietly.

"That's what they told me," she whispered back.

"You don't believe them?"

"We buried a body. They said he was too badly burned and..." She sucked in a breath, fighting back another round of sobs. "They used dental records to identify the bodies."

"Bodies?" Nick asked. "How many?"

"Six counting Miah. His entire team."

"I'm sorry."

"Me too. He was going to be coming home in a few weeks and we were going to be married right after Christmas. He'd put in a request to transfer stateside and start a different type of training."

"Maddie, I don't even know what to say," Nick told her.

She heard the sorrow in his words and slowly turned her head to look at him. He wasn't just saying kind words; he looked as if he could feel her pain. "I've been trying to pretend nothing happened for the last year."

"It's only been a year? Wow, I mean...how much time did you take off work?"

Maddie shrugged her shoulder and tried to shake her head. "I didn't really take that much time. I needed to keep busy."

"Family?"

"His mom and mine, but neither of them live here any longer. I haven't spoken to Mrs. Shaw since the funeral." She looked at him and tried to explain, "I know that probably makes me sound like a horrible person, but she calls every week and leaves these messages about how she's praying for me and how Jeremiah wouldn't want me to be sad and would want me to move on with my life. It's like she went to the funeral and then immediately jumped back into living her life."

"I'm sure that's not the case," Nick offered.

Maddie took a breath and said, "I'm sure it's not, but...I couldn't figure out how to talk to her without admitting Miah was never coming home."

"So, what changed?" Nick asked, his hands hanging between his knees.

She fixed her eyes on his long fingers, wishing they were still holding her. She still felt as if she would crack any minute; crack into a million pieces that couldn't be put back together.

"Maddie?"

She looked at him and felt fresh tears spill down her cheeks. "They closed the cemetery to do some work and then the snow came, so the work hasn't been completed, and I don't know when they're going to open the gate again. I can't talk to him..."

"Wait, why can't you talk to him? Do you really think you have to be in the cemetery and by a grave marker before that can happen?"

Maddie looked at him, confusion marring her brow. Her head was pounding, and she felt like there was something important she needed to say, but she couldn't think...

"My head hurts."

"I'm sure crying didn't help. Let me go get you some more painkillers, and then you need to eat something." Nick left for a moment and returned with several pills and a glass of water. "Take these. I have a sandwich for you and some soup."

Maddie gratefully swallowed the pills. Nick suddenly swept her off the sofa and carried her to the bar where he'd set their food.

"I could have walked."

"Or you could have tried and fallen. This way, you didn't risk injuring yourself further. I didn't have to watch you injure yourself, and we both get to eat."

Maddie swallowed and then focused on eating the food. She was surprised that she was hungry. She finished both the sandwich and the soup, along with another cup of tea. Sleep was calling her, but she had to deny it for a few more hours, at a minimum. She cradled her head on her hand as Nick quietly removed their dishes. Nature took that time to call, and she regretted drinking both the water and the tea.

She picked her heavy head up and asked, "Where's your bathroom?"

"Down the hall, but the tile is really slick. Let me help you."

"That's okay..."

Nick was having none of it. Once again, he carried her down the hallway. He stood her up at the sink in the bathroom and then met her eyes in the mirror. "Are you going to be okay? Not dizzy or anything?"

"I'll be fine," she told him, refusing to admit the world around her was spinning crazily. She could manage to go to the bathroom without help.

"I'll be right outside the door. Holler when you're finished, and I'll take you back to the couch."

"I can walk..."

"Not today, you can't. Doctor's orders," Nick told her firmly.

"You're not my doctor," she informed him.

"Good thing, too. I would have demanded you spend the night in the hospital for observation." Nick gave her a smile. "Besides, I thought we already covered the fact that today I'm your friend."

"I don't need the hospital. I just bumped my head..."

"No, you wrecked your car. Rather splendidly, I might add."

"Geez, don't remind me. I need to call the insurance company..."

"Already taken care of."

"How? When?"

"While you were getting your CT scan and by me. I found your insurance card in your wallet. I gave them all the details. Whenever you're up to driving again, you can pick up a rental while your car is being fixed." He paused and then added, "Provided it's fixable."

"It was that bad?" she asked, not remembering much from the accident.

"You rolled at least once, maybe more. There didn't seem to be many panels on the vehicle that were undamaged."

"Great," she muttered.

"Don't worry about that right now. You're not driving for a few days, at least until you get a medical clearance. Until then, I'm happy to play chauffeur."

Maddie let out a breath and then gave him a tight smile. "Thanks. Now, if you'll leave..."

"Going. Remember, I'm right outside the door."

Maddie managed to sit on the toilet without falling in or sliding off. Once she was finished, she even managed to wash and dry her hands before feeling as if an entire load of bricks had been dumped on her. Exhaustion hit her so suddenly, she had to grip the vanity to keep from collapsing. She gave it a good minute, hoping her strength would return and she could manage to get herself out of the bathroom without help, but she only felt more and more unsteady.

Setting any thoughts of heroics aside, she weakly called out, "Nick? I could probably use some help right about now."

The door opened and Nick's hands were suddenly on her waist, giving her support. "Are you finished in here?"

She nodded and then winced. "Ouch!"

"Back to the couch with you." He swept her up in his arms and carefully exited the bathroom, making sure she didn't hit her head on the door jamb or the railing. "Here we go," he murmured as he deposited her on the couch once again.

Maddie sighed as her body sank into the overstuffed cushions. She was exhausted, both from her tears and from the horrific day she'd endured. Tomorrow would bring with it a whole bevy of new concerns to be dealt with. They would have to wait until she had gotten some rest before she could even consider dealing with them.

She let her eyes close partway, watching Nick as he got a fire going in the hearth and then grabbed a blanket from a basket and draped it over her body.

"Thank you," she murmured quietly.

"No thanks needed. Want me to sit with you for a while?"

"Can I go to sleep yet?"

"Not for a few more hours. We could watch a movie..."

"That sounds painful," she replied.

"So, no movie. How about I just sit here, and I'll tell you all about my childhood?"

"As long as you don't expect me to reciprocate..."

"Maybe not today, but soon. I want to know all about you. I'm brave enough to start."

She tried to stay awake, but it seemed impossible. Nick annoyed her for the next few hours, talking louder than was necessary and even going so far as to tickle her feet. He continued to ask her questions, verifying that she still knew her name, the date, and who was President.

Finally, after he'd come up with several ways of slowly torturing her to death, he declared she was doing well and could go to sleep for a few hours. He promised to wake her up periodically throughout the night to ensure she was still operating on all cylinders, but she didn't care about that. She closed her eyes, snuggled down into the couch cushions with the soft blanket and allowed her mind to enter that sweet place called oblivion.

Chapter 16

The next afternoon...

Maddie was going stir crazy. Only one day had passed since she'd become an unwilling invalid with a large bruise on her head and a concussion. Not doing anything was slowly making her edgy and anxious. She'd tried to convince Nick that she was capable of going to work today, but he'd adamantly refused. While she'd been dozing on his couch, he'd showered and dressed in scrubs. He'd woken her up on his way out of the door, not even giving her a chance to try and convince him she was feeling much better.

He'd left three hours earlier with a promise to return as soon as he could, but that it might be a long day. He had lots of patients undergoing various procedures today, and he wouldn't leave the hospital until he was sure everyone was out of recovery and doing well. He had another physician covering for him, but he wanted to be there for his patients and their families. Maddie had assured him she was more than capable of staying by herself for a few hours.

Maddie really liked Nick's commitment to his patients; she only wished he didn't consider her one of them. She had things to do and places to be...her apartment, the body shop, the cemetery.

She glanced at the clock one more time and then tightened her lips and reached for her cell phone. She called a local taxi company and was assured that someone would be at her present location within half an hour and would be more than willing to hang with her for the rest of the afternoon.

She did what she could with her hair, pulling some strands forward so that they partially hid the dark bruise and swelling just above her right eyebrow. The girls on the floor had thought ahead enough to grab her some extra scrubs from her locker, so she at least had a clean set of clothing to put on. She'd slept in one of Nick's t-shirts and a pair of sweatpants that she'd needed to roll up half a dozen times at the waist. Going out in public dressed like that wasn't even a consideration.

When the taxi pulled up, she stepped outside and pulled the door closed but then paused. She briefly debated the wisdom of leaving the door unlocked. This was a fairly safe neighborhood, and she hoped to be back before Nick came home. After the emotional rollercoaster of last night, she had a burning desire to visit Miah's gravesite. Yes, she could actually think of it that way now. Miah was dead. He wasn't coming back, but she wasn't quite ready to let go of him. Visiting the cemetery had become a habit that she wasn't sure she could just up and quit.

Deciding to leave the front door unlocked, she hurried to the taxi and inwardly vowed to make this visit as quick as possible. She needed to talk to Miah. Desperately.

"Memorial Gardens Cemetery, please," she told the driver as she slipped into the backseat.

"Sure thing. You know it's been closed for over a week now."

"I'm aware of that fact. Are the roads still pretty bad?"

"They're a little slick," he told her as he pulled out onto the main road. "Don't you worry, none. I'll get you there in one piece."

"Thanks. I won't be very long...I was hoping maybe you could wait for me and bring me right back here?"

He looked at her in the rearview mirror and then replied, "I'd have to leave the meter running..."

"That's fine. Oh! Uhm...I only have a card..."

"That's fine. They've equipped us all with this nifty little thing that hooks right onto our cell phones."

Maddie nodded, trying not to grimace at the way her head was starting to pound. *I probably should have talked myself out of this, rather than allowing my emotions to get the better of me. God, give me the strength to do this.*

. . ⚜ . .

MEMORIAL GARDENS CEMETERY...

Charity watched as the taxi pulled up to the cemetery and then slowly rolled through the gate. The roadway had been freshly cleaned of snow and ice. She'd been hovering over Maddie since her accident, especially after yesterday's emotional outburst. She was so close to a breakthrough, but Charity was afraid that, left to her own devices, she would fall right back into the familiar trap of ignoring her grief.

"Take the first right and then stop at the second tree," Maddie told the driver.

"Sure thing."

Moments later, the taxi came to a stop and Maddie slipped from the rear door. "I won't be long," she called back inside to the driver before slamming the door shut. She pulled her coat around her and then headed for Miah's gravesite with her head tucked against the wind.

Charity hovered over her right shoulder, picking up a myriad of emotions. By the time Maddie reached the well-worn spot in front of Miah's gravesite, she had tears streaming down her cheeks. She'd remembered her gloves this time and brushed the ice and snow off of the headstone, not stopping until it was as clean and as pristine as she could make it under the current weather conditions.

"Hey, Miah. Sorry I haven't been able to come see you. They actually shut the cemetery and wouldn't let anyone drive through the gates. We've had a lot of snow and... Well, I tried to come see you yesterday. It didn't go so well. I wrecked my car. I'm okay...I will be okay. My head really hurts right now. I have a concussion and a few bruises, but I'll be fine in a few days."

She paused and took several deep breaths. She watched her breath, the white tendrils rising up to the sky as she released it. Charity could feel the confusion in Maddie's mind, but she resisted the urge to soothe her charge. A little confusion might push her to show her true emotions. Maddie's ability to control her emotions is what had gotten her to this point without having to deal with the reality of Miah's death. She needed to move forward.

"Miah," Maddie paused as her emotions bubbled to the surface. "I hate that you left me. You were supposed to come home, and we were supposed to get married and have this beautiful life. You ruined it." She was openly sobbing now, her tears dropping off her chin and falling to the snow.

Maddie dropped to her knees and wrapped her arms around her middle as her grief exploded. "I've been coming here, trying to pretend that somehow we didn't really bury you. I know you're never coming back..."

Angels weren't supposed to cry, but the raw grief in Maddie's whispered words brought moisture to Charity's eyes. She hovered closer, sending comfort and grace toward Maddie and wishing for a way to ease the young woman's burden. This was something that needed to occur if she was ever to be whole again.

Maddie cried for several long minutes; her body bent in half as she tried to contain the hurt. "I've been so angry with you and with myself...I can't believe I was angry at a...a...a dead man."

Maddie sobbed some more, and Charity wished there was some way she could help her. She was debating the wisdom of planting a few thoughts in her head, just to help ease her burden of guilt, when suddenly she felt another presence behind her. She turned her head and saw Matthias watching her with a very wary look upon his face.

"Matthias."

"Charity. Please tell me you weren't interfering with human emotions."

Charity shook her head, "I was only thinking about it. I didn't act upon those thoughts, I just…look at her! She's feeling guilty because she was angry with her fiancé for dying."

"Ah. And you were thinking a few thoughts might help her?"

"I was thinking that…yes. But…I didn't do anything."

"May I inquire why not?" Matthias asked, a stern look upon his face.

"Well, besides the fact that it would break the Guardian Angel Code…I was really hoping that she'd be able to get past this on her own. I mean, she's making some progress. At least she's actually mentioning that Jeremiah died and expressing her feelings. Those are good things, yes?"

Matthias nodded and then turned his head. He pointed to where another vehicle was pulling up behind the waiting taxi. Charity's eyes went wide. *Nick!* She had not seen this coming.

Maddie was too immersed in her grief and didn't notice his arrival, either. Nick slowly got out of his car, quietly paid the driver, and sent him on his way. He then went back to his own car and leaned against the passenger side, giving Maddie privacy and a chance to speak her mind without feeling self-conscious or embarrassed.

"How did he know she was here?" Charity asked Matthias.

"Call it intuition. Don't do anything I wouldn't approve of," and with that he was gone.

Charity sighed and then turned her attention back to Charity. Nick had come looking for her. If his arrival moved Maddie closer to finding solace and healing, she didn't care about the how, just the outcome.

Chapter 17

Nick tucked his hands into the pocket of his coat and watched the young woman who was single-handedly turning his life upside down. Before he'd left for the hospital several hours earlier, he'd told her he might be gone most of the day. After doing an initial check on his patients, something had told him he needed to head home and check on Maddie. She'd suffered a concussion and, while she didn't seem to be suffering from anything more than the normal headache and muscle stiffness after her emotional shedding the night before, he felt like he needed to keep an eye on her.

He still couldn't believe that she'd been ignoring her grief for more than a year. Nick knew her work history. She had been working at the hospital when her fiancé had been killed, so he was baffled as to how she'd managed to hide what was happening for so long. He'd just happened to run into another physician who had worked with Maddie before she transferred to his floor. They were under the impression that she'd recovered from her great loss rather quickly. Nick hadn't told them how wrong they were.

He'd been turning onto his street just as the taxi had pulled away, but the significance of its presence hadn't dawned on him until he entered his house and found it empty. He'd immediately placed a call to the taxi company, and they'd been more than happy to relay the taxi's destination when he'd explained that the passenger was medically compromised.

The wind shifted, and he pulled his jacket closer around his shoulders. Scrubs were fine for working inside the hospital, but they did nothing to ward off the chill of the winter wind which was currently swirling the snow around the trees. Maddie didn't seem to be immune to the cold, either. He watched as she pulled her coat closer about her body. Deciding her health was more important that whatever was taking place at her fiancé's gravesite, he pushed off the SUV and headed to where she knelt in the snow.

"Maddie?" he quietly called to her when she didn't give any appearance of having heard him approaching. She lifted her head and looked at him with teary eyes. Confusion marred her brow, and he could tell her head was hurting.

"Nick?" She looked back to where the taxi had been waiting and then frowned more. "How?"

"I came back home because I was worried about you."

"Your patients..." she murmured.

"Don't worry about them today." Nick lifted her to her feet. "Right now, it's you I'm concerned about. It's really cold out here and your cheeks are bright red. Head hurt?"

Maddie nodded shortly. "This wasn't my best idea..."

Nick wrapped an arm around her shoulders and started leading her back to his vehicle. "I thought maybe you were heading back to your apartment. I was kind of surprised that your first stop was here."

"I needed to talk to Miah..."

"And you can only do that here?" Nick asked, opening up the passenger door and ushering her inside the warmth of the vehicle. He turned the car back on and adjusted the heat. A few moments later, reaching across her, he fastened her seatbelt before sitting back and just watching her.

"You never answered my question. Do you think you can only talk to Miah here? At the cemetery?"

Maddie looked down at her hands for a long moment before she shrugged one shoulder and gave a half nod. "I guess."

"Hmm. Let me ask you another question, then. Do you believe in God?"

She looked up at him and nodded. "Yes. Why?"

"Well, do you only talk to God when you're inside of a church?"

"Of course not." She took a breath and then settled back against the seat. "I get where you're going with this, but it's different."

"How so? You're too smart to think that Miah's spirit is in that grave."

"No, he was a believer and he's in Heaven," she replied softly.

"So..." He just let the sentence hang as he pulled out of the cemetery and headed back home. After speaking with his colleague earlier, he was certain that Maddie had been repressing her sorrow for the last year instead of dealing with her loss and trying to move forward with her life. George, the security guard, confirmed his suspicion. It seemed his brother-in-law was the head gardener at the cemetery and had been very worried about Maddie over the previous few months.

"I suppose you think I should just talk to Miah anywhere?" she asked.

"Well, that was one thought," Nick told her, wishing he knew the right words to help her.

She shook her head and then moaned in pain. She closed her eyes and Nick watched the way her brow furrowed as she struggled with what had to be a pounding headache. "You need to lie down and take some more pain medication."

"I needed to talk to Miah more," she countered back.

"Do you mind me asking why? What was so important that you jeopardized your own health and recovery to go to the cemetery today?"

"I...I needed to tell him..."

She started to cry, and Nick inwardly chided himself for pushing her. He pulled the vehicle over and turned off the engine. "Maddie, talk to me."

"I...I'm so angry," she choked out amidst her tears.

"At God?"

"Yes. And Miah! He left me! And I wasted an entire year because I couldn't face that fact."

Nick said nothing for a moment, and then tried to get her mind to think more clearly about the matter. "Do you think your fiancé wanted to get blown up?"

"No!" she told him in anguish. "I don't think he wanted to get blown up, but he did."

"And that is his fault?" Nick asked, giving her plenty of time to process his question.

She shook her head and sobbed quietly, holding her head in pain. "I...we had everything all planned out and then...it was just...gone. His mother was all alone. I was all alone..."

"Wait, you weren't all alone. You had family and friends here to support you."

"I wouldn't let them," she murmured, wiping her face with her hands.

"Why not?"

"They always wanted to talk about Miah and how I was doing. I didn't want to be constantly reminded of what I'd lost. I just wanted to pretend that he was still on tour and...I didn't want to say goodbye to him. It hurt too badly."

"So, you pretended he wasn't really gone?" Nick asked, wondering if he needed to get Maddie some kind of counseling to help her process things correctly.

"I know what you're thinking," she challenged him. "You're thinking I've got some psychological problem and need professional help, but I don't. It hurt so bad the day I watched them put his casket in the ground, and a few days later, I had this dream and it was so real...Miah was coming across the tarmac and I jumped into his arms...I decided I liked that version better than reality. As long as I stayed in that dream, I could function and do my job. I think I knew I was only prolonging things, but it was easier..."

"Than dealing with the truth," Nick finished for her. "But you knew all along he wasn't coming home?"

"I did. That's why I came to the cemetery every morning and again each night. I kept thinking that one day I'd come here, and magically it wouldn't hurt so badly. I'd be ready to move on. I was wrong."

"Maddie, you've counselled enough parents and family members to know it doesn't work that way. There is no short cut around the grieving process."

She nodded and then looked at him. "I know. I've known that for a while now, but... going along with the status quo didn't require any changes. Zachary helped me see that."

"Zachary?" Nick asked in surprise.

"He's lost more than I have, and yet, he's looking forward to the future. Did you know he really wants to play baseball?"

"I didn't know that."

"What's going to happen to him? Is he..."

"He's in full remission. His last chemo treatment was just a precautionary to make sure there were no rogue cells wandering around."

Maddie gave him a teary smile and nodded. "That's wonderful news. Have you told him?"

"Not yet. I'm still waiting on some more lab results." Nick sighed and then placed his hands on the steering wheel. "I was hoping to have his future all worked out but there's a problem."

"What kind of problem?" Maddie asked.

"I don't want to burden you with the details," he told her.

"I thought we were friends," she reminded him.

Nick gave her a look and then nodded with a chuckle. "So we are. Are you sure you're up to listening to my problem?"

"Well, I've heard all about how your parents tricked you into pulling your first tooth. How you accidentally let the frogs out of their cage in fourth grade. How you used your mother's pasta strainer to look for gold in the back yard, and that you named your cat dissection specimen Fluffy and angered most of the girls in the classroom."

"How was I to know that several of them had cats? I only had dogs growing up."

Maddie hid a smirk at the confusion marring his brow. "I'm sure they've forgiven you by now."

"I hope so. I have a reunion coming up this summer and, to be honest, I'm not sure I even want to attend."

"I'm sure it'll be fine."

"Maybe. Wanna go with me?" Nick asked offhandedly.

"What?" Maddie asked.

"Want to go with me? To my reunion? Really, I hate the idea of going back alone."

"You can't take me to your high school reunion," she argued.

"Why not?"

"Well..."

"Exactly. You can't come up with a good excuse."

"How about we deal with more immediate problems and leave summer until at least March?" Maddie suggested.

"Fine."

"Good. So tell what the problem with Zachary is."

"It seems in order for me to petition for full custody of Zachary, his grandmother has to sign off on the paperwork. She was named his legal guardian in Jeff's will."

"But...I thought she had Alzheimer's? Doesn't that render her incapable of making those types of decisions?"

"Normally, it would. Not in Louisiana. She has to be declared mentally incompetent before that goes into effect there."

"And she hasn't reached that stage of her illness yet," Maddie surmised.

"No. I'm trying to convince her to come out here for Christmas so that she can see Zachary and understand how much better off he would be here with me."

"Is she capable of traveling that far by herself?" Maddie asked.

"Physically she is, but I'm not so sure she could handle the mental energy such a trip would require. Not by herself. I thought about just buying her a ticket, but I'm afraid she'd just ignore it or think that I'm trying to be heavy handed." Nick started up the vehicle again and said, "Let's get you back home and give your brain a small rest."

Maddie said nothing. It wasn't until he was pulling into his garage that she spoke up again. "Have Zachary call her."

"What?" he asked, turning off the engine and shutting the garage door.

"Zachary thinks she left him here and misses her. Have him call her and ask her to come here. Better yet, have him video chat with her. I'm sure her daughter or someone in her family has a device that would support a video call. Let her see for herself that he's doing better."

"But he doesn't look better. He's lost a lot of weight since she left two months ago."

Maddie gave him a small smile. "And hopefully she'll be concerned enough to get on a plane and come out to see how he is for herself."

Nick stared at her and then slowly smiled. "That's kind of devious, but it just might work. She was very upset when I refused to transfer Zachary's medical care to someone back in Louisiana. Even though Zachary looks sick, his test results and his zest for life could convince anyone that he's on the mend."

"Glad I could help." She opened the car door and then sat for a minute.

"You okay?" Nick asked, placing a hand on her shoulder when she appeared to be weaving a bit.

"Dizzy and hurting."

"Stay there and I'll help you inside." Nick hurried around the car and then kept one arm around her waist as he led her back into the house and the couch that she'd occupied the night before.

Maddie leaned against him, hyper aware of the attraction that was building between them. Nick seemed to take every opportunity to touch her. Her arm. Her shoulder. Carrying her when she was more than capable of walking. It was unsettling and also exciting. Given her current emotional state, she wasn't sure if she should trust her feelings or just try to ignore them.

She stumbled on the throw rug leading from the kitchen into the rest of the house and, seconds later, her feet left the floor as Nick's arms cradled her.

"You're beginning to make this a habit," she said.

"Complaining?" he asked with a grin.

Maddie sighed and relaxed in his hold. "No. To be honest, I seem to be clumsier than usual."

"Your balance is still messed up. It'll return if you get plenty of rest."

"A nap sounds good."

After getting her settled in, he retrieved her pills and a glass of water. "One pill or two?"

"Just one."

Maddie swallowed the pill and then closed her eyes while she waited for it to take effect. He rubbed the back of her hand with his thumb. As the pain began to receded, she cracked her eyes open and murmured, "Thank you."

Nick searched her eyes and then leaned forward and kissed her forehead. "Sleep now," he whispered to her before getting up and adjusting the blanket from the back of the couch over her.

He retrieved his laptop and sat in a chair across the room to work on updating his patient files and progress notes while she slept. Her suggestion of having Zachary invite his grandmother for Christmas was a brilliant one. He intended to put it into action. He didn't want to leave Maddie alone again. When she woke up, he'd see about taking her with him to the hospital. Hopefully, by the time he called this day over he'd be one step closer to making his and Zachary's futures more secure.

He looked at Maddie and felt his heart soften. It seemed almost impossible that he'd only known her for less than a week. He felt a connection to her that he was finding hard to ignore. The fact that she was obviously still grieving the loss of her first love bothered him, but not so much that he didn't want to see if they had a future together. He might have to wait a while, but in the meantime, he'd take friendship with her over nothing at all. She was good with Zachary and it was obvious the two of them had bonded at a deeper level than any of the other nurses or staff had, except for himself.

Kids were excellent judges of character and Zachary needed as many people in his corner as he could get. He wasn't sure what the future held, but Maddie would have to be a part of it, even if it was only in the form of a friend and mentor to the little boy that he hoped to one day call his adopted son.

I really hope she's going to be more, though. I've never felt this way about a woman before.

Chapter 18

Later that afternoon...

"Are you sure you're up to doing this?" Nick asked for the tenth time since agreeing to let Maddie accompany him to the hospital to check on his patients.

"I'm fine. My headache is barely there right now, and I'm not dizzy at all." In fact, after taking a small nap, Maddie was feeling almost back to normal. Almost. Before heading to the hospital, she'd convinced Nick to take her to her own apartment so that she could get some real clothes. She'd almost managed to get dressed by herself before the phone rang. She'd glanced at the caller I.D. and thought about ignoring it, but then she realized her mother had probably tried to call her the night before for their weekly talk. Her mother would be worried that she hadn't been able to reach her as Maddie was always home in the evenings. The last thing she wanted to do was worry her mother. She hit the speaker button so that she could continue to get ready while she talked.

"Hi, mom," Maddie forced a cheerfulness to her voice she didn't feel. In truth, she was emotionally exhausted after yesterday, but her mother didn't have a clue that she hadn't dealt with Miah's death yet. Maddie intended to keep it that way. She loved her mother, but she tended to lecture rather than just offer her support. While Maddie appreciated the latter, she truly didn't have the mental strength to deal with a lecture right now.

"Maddie. Thank goodness I caught you. What's wrong?"

"Why would you assume something is wrong?" Maddie asked, sitting down on the side of the bed after pulling up her jeans. She managed to finish pushing her arms through the shirt and pulled it down while her mother expounded all of the reasons that she'd been worried.

"I called you last night and you didn't answer. You can't imagine all of the horrible images that went through my head. I even called that hospital where you work and they told me you weren't working today. Are you sick? Is that it? What's wrong? Have you been to the doctor? I haven't checked the flights yet, but I could probably be there sometime later tonight..."

"Mom, stop! I'm fine."

"Well, something's obviously wrong. What is it?"

Maddie inwardly sighed, knowing her mother wasn't going to just let her sweep things under the rug. Maddie had broken her normal routine by not being there the evening before to answer the phone and that had her mother's radar pinging loudly. She closed her eyes for a moment as her headache made itself known and explained in the least dramatic way possible.

"I had a slight accident yesterday."

"Accident? What do you mean, accident? Did you fall?"

"No. I was driving."

"Did you fall asleep? I've warned you about working such long hours..."

"No, mom. It was morning. I wrecked because the roads were really slick, and I slid off the road. The weather has been really bad here. Anyway, I bumped my head, but I'm fine."

"They kept you in the hospital overnight? How come I wasn't contacted? Maddie did you change your emergency contact person?"

"Mom, please stop. I didn't change anything. I have a slight concussion, but they didn't keep me at the hospital. I spent the night at a friend's house just as a precaution."

"Oh my. A concussion? Maddie...I'll fly out..."

"I don't need you to come out here, mom. Although, I appreciate the gesture, I'm fine I'll be back to work tomorrow."

I'm not sure how I'm going to get there yet, but I'm going to work tomorrow. Another day left alone with my thoughts might just finish me off. I need to focus on something...anything...besides the sorry mess I've made of my personal life.

"...call Brenda. She's not very far away and I'm sure..."

"I don't want you to call Brenda," Maddie told her firmly. She still hadn't decided what to do about the heap of guilt resting on her shoulders where Miah's mom was concerned. The woman had only been kind and compassionate toward her and Maddie had been rude and uncommunicative. Pushing aside those thoughts for another time, she dealt with her mom.

"I got into a little fender bender and bumped my head. Given the crappy weather conditions we've had here lately, I'm not surprised. I'll get the car fixed and everything will be back to normal in no time."

"Oh, your little car," he mother sympathized. "Is it badly damaged?"

"I'm waiting to hear back from the shop. In the meantime, my insurance is providing me a rental car. So, you see, everything's fine."

"If you're sure..."

"I'm positive. Now, tell me what's new with you. Last week you mentioned you might have plans for Christmas. I know you were planning on me coming out there, but I just can't take time away from work right now. I started working up on the third floor in pediatrics and I really like it there."

"That's wonderful, Maddie. I'm happy for you. I remember you mentioning a desire to work up there before...well, I'm glad you got the opportunity."

"Me too. Now, you didn't answer my question. What's new with you?"

"Well...uhm..."

Maddie raised a brow at her mother's hesitation. "Mom? You're starting to scare me."

"Oh, that's not...I'm good."

"So, there's nothing you need to tell me?"

"Well...I..."

Maddie frowned at the hesitancy in her mother's voice and then smirked. Her mother was trying to hide something from her, but that hadn't work when she was fourteen and it definitely wasn't going to work now. "Spill it mom. What's going on?"

"I joined a singles club for people my age and I'm going on a cruise over Christmas."

Her mother said the words in a rushed fashion, leaving Maddie speechless for a long moment. *She joined a singles' club? My mother? Wow! Okay. That's not what I was expecting to hear, but...way to go mom!*

Maddie made sure she had her emotions under control before she spoke again. There was a smile on her face when she replied, "That's awesome. Have you met anyone yet?" When her mother stumbled a bit before replying, Maddie's smile grew bigger.

"Well...I just started going a few months ago..."

"But...you didn't answer my question. You met someone, didn't you? What's his name?" Maddie chuckled when her mother sputtered on the other end of the line.

"His name?"

"Yes. What's the man's name who has you blushing like a schoolchild?"

"How do you know I'm blushing?" her mother queried right back.

"Can you tell me you're not?" Maddie fired back. "Come on, tell me his name."

"Uhm...well, his name is Kevin. He's a retired banker and lost his wife to cancer several years ago. He's very nice and...I think you'd like him."

"I'll look forward to meeting him," Maddie told her. "Has he asked you out yet?"

"We've gone for coffee and dinner a couple of times."

"A couple of times? Mom, you've been holding out on me," Maddie teased her.

"Er...I didn't want to say anything...:

"Why not? I'm happy for you. It's way past time you found some friends to hang out with and maybe a new love interest. Dad's been gone for a really long time. You need to move on."

"Oh, it's not like that."

"Then it should be." A sound at the bedroom door had her turning to see Nick standing there, leaning against the doorjamb, a bemused smile upon his face. How long he'd been standing there, she wasn't quite sure, but it was obvious he'd heard some of her conversation. "Mom, someone's here so I need to go."

"Are you sure you're okay?"

"I'm fine. Promise. Have fun on your cruise and I want to hear all about it when you get back."

"Maddie...I'm sorry...I know this year must be tough..."

Maddie's face felt frozen as she shutdown her emotions. "Please don't go there. Everything is fine."

"But Miah..."

"Is gone and I'm dealing with it."

"Are you? Are you really dealing with it?" her mother asked. "Brenda and I talk, you know. You really should take her calls. She's worried about you."

Maddie swallowed and ignored Nick's questioning look. "I'll take care of it, okay. I've been busy and...you know."

"I do know," her mother assured her. "When your father died, I wanted to curl up in a ball in our bedroom and never come back out. But life went on, and I had you to take care of and, before I knew it, I was laughing and smiling again. Can you say the same?"

For all her mother was or wasn't, she had an uncanny ability to see right through Maddie's pretenses. The fact that she had allowed them to continue so long was amazing. Maddie took a deep breath and then closed her eyes. "I'm working through things. It's just...well, I needed some time."

"Maddie, why don't I come out there for Christmas? There will be another cruise..."

"No, mom. Go on your cruise and enjoy yourself. This is something I have to do on my own and I promise you, I am dealing with it. And I'll call Brenda before Christmas."

"Are you sure, sweetie?"

"I'm positive mom. Have a great time and don't forget your sunblock. The sun will be brutal on the water."

"I'll be extra careful. I love you," her mother told her.

"I know. I love you, too. Merry Christmas." Maddie disconnected the call before her mother could try and keep the conversation going. Nick was waiting on her.

Chapter 19

After a moment, Maddie looked up and met Nick's eyes, feeling the need to try and explain some of what he'd overheard. "That was my mom. She moved down to Florida a couple of years ago. She hates the snow."

Nick nodded. "Living in Montana during the winter would probably not be her thing, then."

"Not at all. She came out here last year for Christmas a few weeks early...She'd just gotten here a few days before I found out about Miah..."

Nick nodded. "She doesn't know what's been going on."

Maddie shook her head and then shrugged her shoulders. "I didn't think so, but now...I think she's probably put it altogether and has some idea of what I haven't been doing. But that's over now. It's definitely time to move on."

Nick raised an eyebrow and asked, "That's kind of a sudden change of heart, isn't it? You didn't seem to be in that mind frame last night."

"It's time. Miah's not coming back." She swallowed hard over the words. "That's the first time I've really acknowledged that out loud."

She looked down for a moment and then swallowed and grabbed hold of her new mindset. "No matter how deep I bury my head in the sand, that fact isn't going to change. I've known that all along, but...yesterday at the cemetery, before I wrecked, I told Miah some things. I told God a few things too. And then today...well, I'm angry at both of them. I know that's an irrational response, but there it is. I'm angry. I'm mad." She paused and then added, "And I'm angry at myself for letting things get to this point."

"So, what are you going to do about it?" Nick asked.

"Start living again. I mean, I've been going through the motions, and ...you know, this is partly your fault."

"How do you figure that?" Nick asked with an arched brow.

"The way you run the third floor."

"What does that have to do with what you're dealing with?" Nick asked curiously.

"Well...it's so different than any other area of the hospital. So many of those kids have been given a death sentence. Just look at Melanie, and Sarah...Zachary."

"Each of those kids is dealing with something completely different. Melanie has leukemia and Sarah had a tumor on her kidney…"

"I know their diseases are all different, but that's not what I was talking about. The third floor doesn't seem like a hospital."

"They get excellent medical care…"

"I wasn't taking issue with that. I fully agree. You provide those kids and their families the best oncology care they can get. I remember reading an article about your success rate and it's twice the national average."

Nick said nothing and looked slightly uncomfortable with her praise. That was something else she'd noticed about him. He treated the workers on the third floor as part of one large team, from the nurses all the way down to the janitorial staff – everyone shared in the successes of the third-floor patients.

"The only thing I can personally take responsibility for is choosing the right people to make up my team. You're now part of that and I have to say, I really like some of the novel ideas you've brought with you. I really want to get them written down and we'll start implementing them right away. I'm still confused though, how is you working on the third floor responsible for this drastic change in your life outlook?"

"It's not really any one thing. Those kids are so sick, and yet, you make sure they spend every minute they have left living life to the fullest. You don't just recommend it to their families, you make sure it happens all around them. It's like being immersed in a big bowl of life, but only the happy and fun things have been included."

"Thanks."

Maddie continued, wanting to try and put into words the change that had occurred in her. "I've been closed off for the last year, not really letting anything affect me. I've come to work and done my job, but it's like I've been inside of a bubble. I never really allowed anything to penetrate the wall I'd put up around my emotions. But those kids…I've seen firsthand the tremendous struggles they are dealing with.

"Some of them have such a long road to recovery ahead of them, and then others…they know the chances of them surviving their cancer is minimal, but they never give up. I tried keeping my distance, but it's impossible to stay emotionally detached in the face of their optimism and zest for life."

"That's the idea," Nick told her quietly. "Happy kids have hope and hope keeps them fighting. Studies have shown that people fighting debilitating illnesses improve faster and respond to treatments more successfully when they aren't depressed, and they have something to look forward to."

"Congratulations. You've definitely accomplished that. I don't know...it's kind of like I've been just moving through this grey world and now it's full of color."

"And possibility," Nick added.

Maddie nodded. "Yeah. Exactly. I still have some things to work through in my head, but I'll get there."

"I know you will," he agreed with her.

"Anyway..." she let the word fade away as she looked at him. He was quickly becoming someone special to her. She admired his work ethic and his commitment to his patients, but it was more than that. From the first moment she'd met him, there had been this invisible bond forming between them that she couldn't explain.

When she'd heard his voice yesterday, while trapped in the car, a sense of relief had come over her. She'd known that somehow Nick was going to help make everything alright. That feeling had continued throughout the day, and even when she'd found him at the cemetery. It hadn't felt...wrong. It had somehow felt right having him by her side.

How weird is that? I mean, I don't really know him, and he doesn't really know me. We've only worked together for a few days...

"Thank you," she told him quietly.

Nick smiled at her and then reached a hand up and brushed the hair back from her temple where a large black and blue bruise still was very visible. "For what?"

"For being there. For caring. For listening," she told him, looking up only to become trapped in his gaze.

"I do care and I will always be there to listen."

Maddie felt her heart skip a beat when his hand slipped down and slid behind her neck. "What's happening here?" she whispered.

Nick searched her eyes and then lowered his head slowly toward her own. "I don't know but I'd like to find out. Can I kiss you?"

Maddie nodded and then his lips were pressing against her own. It was a chaste kiss as far as kisses went, but she felt it all the way into her bones. When he drew away a few seconds later, she followed him, unable to stop the action. Nick smiled down at her and then kissed her again. She gave into the urge to wrap her arms around him and slid her arms over his shoulders.

Kissing Nick felt so natural and, when they broke apart a minute later, it was if the entire world was a brighter place. Her heart was racing and her breath coming a little unsteady, but she didn't care. Kissing Nick had been everything she'd ever wanted in a first kiss and not known that she'd even wanted with him. Surprising. Wonderful. And definitely something that needed repeating.

Nick cleared his throat, drawing physically away from her and giving her a moment to regain her bearings. "Wow!"

"Yeah," she told him with a blush covering her cheeks.

He smiled and then held out his hand for her small overnight bag. "Ready to go?" He'd insisted she pack a bag and spend at least one more night on his couch. He had a guest room, but the bed had recently been replaced and was currently sitting in boxes, having never been put together. Nick had offered to do so later today, but Maddie had assured him that his couch was more than adequate for one more night and he didn't need to go to any special lengths for her. He'd done enough.

Nick didn't happen to agree with her. He'd checked her vitals this morning and not been completely happy with her improvement. Her pupils were still not reacting normally and with her headache, he wasn't willing to take any chances with her recovery. He'd seen people with lesser concussions suffer days later with everything from repetitive headaches to memory loss. He was committed to doing everything possible to make sure Maddie made a full recovery.

In her fragile emotional state, Maddie had inwardly been relieved to know that she wouldn't have to spend the night alone with her thoughts. That day was coming, but she grasped at the chance of a respite. "I'm ready."

She followed him from her bedroom and then waited while he locked her apartment door. He led her toward the stairs and held her elbow as she carefully navigated both sets of stairs. Once they reached his SUV, he tucked her bag into the backseat and then jogged around to the driver's side. He slid behind the wheel and then paused with his hand on the wheel. "Are you sure you're up for this? I can take you back home and go to the hospital by myself."

"I'm okay," she assured him. "I just have a tiny headache. Does Zach know we're coming?"

"I told him I'd be back to see him this afternoon. I didn't mention you because I wasn't sure if you would be up to this and didn't want to disappoint him. You are going to be his surprise."

Maddie smiled, "I think I like the sound of being someone's surprise."

"Zach will be very happy to see you. I assured him that you didn't forget who he was, but I'm not sure that he believed me."

"Well, let's not keep him waiting," Maddie offered up a smile.

Nick started the vehicle and she sat back as he expertly navigated the early afternoon traffic. She let her thoughts drift here and there, not really giving any one thought too much consideration. So much had changed from two days ago, but Maddie wasn't going to question anything right now. She was just going to go with the flow and try to enjoy what was left of this day.

Chapter 20

Upon their arrival at the hospital, it seemed word had spread about her accident and people she only knew vaguely wished her a speedy recovery. It was a relief half an hour later to reach the third floor, but there she also found herself surrounded by her co-workers.

"Girl, you sure gave us all a good scare yesterday," Marci told her after hugging her briefly.

"Sorry."

"Yeah, maybe you could find another way of getting a day off?" Penny suggested with a chuckle.

Maddie blushed and then nodded. "I'll just put a note on the calendar in the lounge from now on."

Nick smiled and nodded his approval. "That sounds like an idea we could all take to heart. Anything I need to know before we go down to see Zach?"

"The rest of his test results came back."

"And?"

"I didn't take a look at them. There have been quite a few things going on around here."

Nick nodded. "Paula?"

"The hospice nurse stopped by here a few hours ago. Everything is set up at home and she rested comfortably throughout the night. The neighbors really came through for the family."

Maddie listened and then turned to Teresa and asked, "Did I miss something?"

Nick turned toward her. "I'll fill you in on our way to Zach's room. Let's go."

Maddie walked beside him, ignoring the curious looks the others gave them. "What's everyone else know that I missed?"

Nick stopped in the hallway and then ushered her into the small chapel room. "Sit down for a minute."

Maddie did so, bracing herself for bad news. "Okay. Tell me what's happening."

"Paula requested she be allowed to go home."

"Home? But," Maddie shook her head and then regretted the motion. She frowned in pain and asked, "How is she continuing..."

"She's not. Her test results showed that nothing has made a difference in the progression of her cancer in the last six weeks. She's getting weaker and only has a limited number of days left. She wanted to be home for Christmas, and I couldn't say no. I just..."

"I get it," Maddie told him, placing a hand on his forearm. "You wanted to try and give them one last time to be together as a family."

Nick shrugged and she could see the unshed tears in his eyes. "I encouraged her parents to celebrate Christmas early. Her neighbors chipped in, with some help from the staff here on the third floor and hospice to give Paula a Christmas to remember."

"You said she only had days left. Christmas is still almost a week away," Maddie reminded him softly.

"I know," Nick told her, his voice telling of a sorrow he couldn't put words to. After a lengthy pause, he suggested, "Let's go see Zach. I need to deliver some good news about now."

He reached for Maddie's hand and she readily gave it to him, thoughts of how it might look to others and keeping her professional distance long gone. Whether it was her injury or simply the season, she was tired of trying to keep her emotions in check. She wanted to feel. Good or bad, happy or sad. Right now, she was just as ready as Nick to hear some good news for a change.

Nick pushed open the little boy's door and let Maddie precede him into the room. "After you."

"Maddie!" Zachary exclaimed when she walked in.

"Hey, buddy. How are you doing?"

"I'm doing great. But, how's your head? You didn't look so good yesterday," he told her.

"I wasn't feeling that well, either. But I'm doing good today. And I didn't forget who I was."

Zachary grinned at her and then waved at Nick. "Thanks for making sure she remembered."

"Kiddo, she did that all on her own. How's the pain today?"

"Good. I haven't had to take any extra medication today and my throat's all better." Zach still seemed lacking in energy but given how long he'd been sick and the extensive treatment he'd been receiving, that wasn't unexpected.

"Glad to hear it. Are you ready for some good news?" Nick asked, pulling up a chair and sitting at Zach's bedside. He'd waited to share the news of his last test results so that Maddie could be there as well.

"Are they good?"

"The best. No sign of cancer and if you keep doing as well as you are now, you're going to get out of here by Christmas."

Zachary smiled and then his face fell. "But...Christmas?"

Nick glanced at Maddie and then nodded. "Yeah. I thought you'd be happy about that."

"I...are you sure the test results are right?" Zachary asked.

Nick was confused. "I'm sure. You're cancer free right now. Zach, what's going on in that brain of yours?"

"I...if I leave here, where will I go? Grandma left and..."

Nick realized the problem and moved to address it, head on. "Well, I was hoping you'd come stay with me for a while."

"Really?" Zach asked, hoping blossoming in his eyes.

"Really." Nick nodded and then added, "I was thinking maybe we could call your grandma and ask her if she wanted to join us. To help use celebrate your recovery."

"Do you think she'd come?" Zach asked hesitantly.

Maddie stepped forward and pulled him into a hug. "I think you should call and ask her yourself."

Zach hugged her back and then asked, "I thought she was sick?"

"She is, but if we make the proper arrangements, there's no reason she couldn't travel out here for a few days to see you."

Zach thought about that for a minute and then asked, "Would I have to go back with her?"

"Do you want to go back with her?" Nick asked.

"Is it bad if I say no? I love her and my cousins and aunts and uncles...but they all have things to do, and I would just be in the way."

"Oh, sweetheart," Maddie hugged him once more. "You would never be in the way."

"That's how it felt when dad...when he went away."

Nick nodded. "I'm sure it felt that way, but if you wanted to go back and live with them, I think things would be different."

"But...I don't want to go back there," Zachary whined. "I want to stay here. I could live with you. I'd be really quiet, and I don't eat very much."

"I hope that's not true," Nick told him with a mock frown. "I need you to eat lots and lots of food to regain the strength and pounds you lost while in the hospital. You can't play baseball if a strong wind is capable of knocking you over."

"Baseball?" Zach asked with big round eyes.

Nick nodded. "I heard you wanted to play. I think we can make that happen." Seeing the happiness on the little boy's face, he only hoped he wasn't counting his chickens before they hatched. If Zach's grandmother wouldn't sign guardianship over to him, he'd have to consider fighting her in court to be appointed Zachary's legal guardian. He hated the idea of having to do that, but this was too important to just let go. Hopefully, it wouldn't come to that and she'd be reasonable.

"I do. I want to play short stop."

"Well, we'll have to work on some skills then once it warms up and the snow melts. Now, how about we call your grandma and convince her to come out here for Christmas?"

Chapter 21

Zach nodded and Maddie retreated to the extra chair against the opposing wall. She was looking a bit pale, and she rubbed at her temple, telling him she had a headache she was trying to hide. When she caught him staring at her, she gave him a smile and then waved toward the phone in his hand. "What are you waiting for?"

Nick nodded and hit the contact button to place the call and then the speaker button. It rang three times before a raspy voice finally answered. "Hello?"

"Clara? This is Dr. Nick Stavros."

"Nick? Is everything alright with Zachary?"

"Everything is fine. In fact, you're on speaker phone, and he's sitting right here."

"Hi, grandma."

"Zachary. It's so good to hear your voice. You sound good."

"I'm feeling good too, grandma. Dr. Nick says I'm going to get to leave the hospital before Christmas."

"Really? Nick, is that true?"

"It sure is. His last test results confirmed that, for now, he's cancer free. We'll continue to test him every three months, or more frequently as needed, to make sure things stay that way, but for now, he's in full remission."

"Oh!" Clara started sobbing on the other end of the line. After a few moments, she pulled herself together enough to finish the call. "I've prayed so hard for this."

"We all have. Anyway, how are you feeling?"

"I have my good and bad times, but the doctors started me on some new medications, and I'm having more good days right now."

"That's wonderful to hear. Zachary has something to ask you." Nick nodded encouragingly at the little boy.

"Grandma, would you come out here and spend Christmas with us?"

"What? Come to Montana? But I assumed you would be coming here. Oh my. Well..."

"Clara, Zachary's not really strong enough to make that kind of trip yet. His immune system is very fragile, and I wouldn't want to risk exposing him to anything by having him get on an airplane."

"Oh, of course. That makes sense. But...well, I've never flown by myself."

"I would take care of making sure there was someone at each stop to help you get from one gate to another. I have plenty of room so you can stay with me while you're here."

"Please, grandma. Will you come spend Christmas with me?"

"Well...I...yes," Clara exclaimed. Nick thought he detected a hint of tears in her voice, but he didn't ask about them. Nick felt so thankful that she and Zachary would be together. He glanced over to where Maddie sat, unshed tears in her eyes as she listened to their conversation. He couldn't tell if they were happy or sad tears, and he made a mental note to ask her about them once they were out of Zachary's room.

"I can't wait to see you," Zachary told his grandmother.

"That goes double for me," Clara replied.

"I'll make all of the arrangements and send them over to your daughter. Are you still living with her?" Nick asked.

"Yes. I'm afraid I'm just not able to live alone any longer."

Nick was already aware of that fact. A few weeks after returning to Louisiana, Clara had put a pie in the over to bake and then forgotten about it. She'd settled in for a nap, but she'd been awakened hours later by the fire alarm going off. When asked about the incident, she couldn't remember putting the pie in the over or turning the appliance on. Her daughter had moved her into their guest bedroom, and after a few days of observation, she'd called Nick to tell him that the move was going to be permanent. Clara was simply forgetting too many things.

Nick had sent her the names of several experts in treating Alzheimer's in their area and Clara had started a completely new medication regimen. He'd only gotten a few brief reports on her progress, but it looked like the medications were working. Clara wasn't nearly as forgetful. He hoped for everyone involved that she continued to show such good progress.

"Don't worry about a thing. Would you like to talk to Zachary once more?"

"Yes. Zachary, tell me what you'd like for Christmas."

Nick listened as Zachary started to list some things that he was hoping Santa would bring him for Christmas, pleased when he saw Maddie taking note as well. He would have to confer with her later to make sure he hadn't missed anything major. Zachary deserved to have a great Christmas and Nick planned on doing everything he could to make that a reality.

"I guess that's all," Zachary told her. "What do you want for Christmas?"

"Seeing you and knowing that you're feeling better is all I could have asked for," Clara told him.

Nick knew that wasn't the truth, but he appreciated the fact that Clara didn't bring up Jeff. He was sure there would be a time when Zachary would need to talk about the fact that his father wasn't around to celebrate with him, but Nick was selfish and didn't want that to be today. Today, he wanted to rejoice in the miracle that had brought healing to Zachary's body.

"Clara, it's Nick again. Can you be ready to travel in three days?"

"Three days..."

"Nick, this is Sheila. I'm sorry, but I was listening in on the conversation. It saves time later on." There was a small pause and then Shelia added, "I took it off of speaker phone on this end."

"No problem. As you heard, I'd like to fly Clara out here for Christmas."

"I think she would like that. We'll see that she gets to the airport and onto the plane."

"Very good. I'll make the arrangements for her to fly out here on the twenty-first?"

"That sounds good."

"Thank you."

"No, thank you. This is one of the best Christmas presents you could have given her. Losing Jeff..."

"I know," Nick cut her off. "We've all had a tough year, Clara and Zach especially. They need to be together this year."

"I agree, but...I've been wanting to speak to you about..."

Nick picked up his phone and took it off of speakerphone, already having a sense for where this conversation was headed. "Maddie, I'm going to step out into the hallway for a moment."

Maddie nodded in understanding and moved over to sit on the side of Zach's bed. "So, tell me more about this list for Santa..."

Nick waited until the door had closed behind him before he walked to the large window at the end of the hallway. "Sorry about the pause. I didn't want to have this conversation where Zachary could overhear. You were saying?"

Sheila sighed. "Nick, I know Clara intended to have Zachary live with her once he was better, but with things the way that they are right now, I don't think that's even a possibility. I know you, and she have talked and she informed you that Tom and I were going to petition the courts for custody of Zachary in her stead. We've talked, and it's not that we don't want to open our home to him, but both of our kids are in high school now. With mom moving in with us and the future uncertain...what kind of a life is that for a little boy?"

Nick felt a glimmer of hope as he asked, "Are you saying that you would support a petition on my part for custody of Zachary?"

"While it's not up to me, I would certainly do everything I could to persuade mom to sign papers to that effect."

Nick felt tears sting his eyes, and he pinched the bridge of his nose in an effort to stave them off a few moments longer. "I would like nothing more than to become Zachary's legal guardian. I won't actually seek to adopt him because I want him to always remember Jeff and his family...but Zachary means so much to me."

"We love him, never doubt that, but Zachary deserves to have the very best, not leftovers. That didn't come out right, but—"

"I get it. I really do. Any help you can give me convincing Clara to sign the papers, I'd be appreciative of. Now, answer me honestly. Is she capable of flying out here by herself?"

It was quiet for a while and then Sheila spoke sadly, "I wish I could say with certainty that she can, but I just don't know. If she has to change planes and there isn't someone right there to stay with her until she boards the next plane, I don't know that she wouldn't wander off."

"Thank you for being honest about that. Would you be amenable to flying down here with her? I'd pay for you to have a round trip flight right back, and then do the same thing after Christmas."

"Gosh, that's very generous of you, Nick. I have to admit I'd feel much better knowing she wasn't flying on her own."

"So would I," Nick told her. "Do you need to talk to Tom before you let me know?"

"No, I'm sure he'll trust my judgment, I was just thinking...if she changed planes in Denver, she could fly straight into Great Falls from there. I could turn around in Denver and fly back to Louisiana, once I knew she was on the plane."

"Are you sure you wouldn't want to just fly all the way here?"

"Maybe on the way home? With Christmas just a week away, I'm really needed here. If I only took her as far as Denver, I could be back the same day," Sheila told him.

"That's not something I'd thought of, but that would work. I could be here when she gets off the plane." Nick's mind was already spinning with a list of things he needed to get done in order to ensure Zachary and Clara had a Christmas to remember. "Sheila, can I send you the flight details later tonight?"

"Of course. Anytime on the twenty-first is fine with me. I'll also start laying the groundwork for Clara where Zachary is concerned. Don't worry if she seems resistant at first. She'll come around."

"I hope so. Thank you again for all of your help."

"Don't mention it. It's the least I can do when I consider all you've done for Zachary...that little boy lost so much this past year. I'm overjoyed that he's going to live a long and healthy life."

"If I have anything at all to say about it, he's going to grow into an old man." Nick said his goodbyes and disconnected the call. He wanted to scream in excitement, but when he turned around, both Penny and Teresa were standing a few feet away and watching him carefully.

He cleared his throat and pocketed his phone. "Ladies, or should I say elves? What's up?"

"Have you seen Zachary yet?" Teresa inquired.

"Yes. Maddie's in with him right now. Why?"

They shared a look and then Penny took a step forward and lowered her voice. "It's Sarah. We just received word that a kidney became available in Wyoming and it's already on a flight to here."

Nick's hopes soared and then stalled. "But?"

"She's running a fever."

"How high?"

"99.8?" Teresa informed him.

"Get the lab up here, STAT. I want to know where the infection is and whether or not it is going to jeopardize the transplant. Have you told her parents yet?"

"Not yet. We didn't want to get their hopes up if it didn't pan out."

"You call the lab and I'll come down and talk to them. I just need to let Maddie know where I'm going."

The nurses nodded and then disappeared down the hallway. Nick took a calming breath, the rollercoaster of emotions that always came with working in pediatric oncology familiar after so many years. With every celebration came another tragedy. He only hoped today he could celebrate to victories and see Sarah on her way to leaving the hospital shortly after the New Year's arrival. Time would tell and it wasn't on his side.

God, if you have any spare miracles up there, Sara could sure use one about now. Thanks.

Chapter 22

Heavenly Realms...

Charity burst into the schoolroom and looked around, almost frantically. Matthias was standing near the far window and she waved at him as she hurried across the space.

"Matthias, I must talk to you."

He arched one white brow and then gestured toward the chairs. "What is bothering you, little angel?"

"Is Sarah going to get the transplant?" Charity didn't beat around the bush but got right to the point.

"Sarah? I thought your charge's name was Maddie?"

"It is, but Sarah is one of the little girls on the hospital ward where Maddie works. She needs a new kidney, and one has become available. Now, she's running a fever and, if she's getting sick, they can't operate. She needs a miracle right now." She was out of breath when she finally stopped talking.

"Many humans are in need of a miracle right now," Matthias told her.

Charity pursed her lips and then took a calming breath before she spoke again. "I know Sarah is not my charge, but she is very important to Dr. Nick, who also is not my charge. Maddie is, and she will be very upset if anything happens to Sarah. She's making such good progress, and I don't want this situation to set her back."

"But, Sarah is not your charge," Matthias reminded her.

Charity nodded and then paced a few steps away. "I know...I just...so many of those children are sick and dying. Fear and worry are palpable there—"

"Is this assignment becoming too much to handle?" Matthias asked her with grave concern in his eyes.

Charity opened her mouth to respond and then closed it, giving serious consideration to his question. *Was being around so much need causing her to lose sight of her goals and her responsibility towards Maddie? It seemed that everything*

135

happening on the third floor of the hospital was intertwined in some way, and no matter the outcomes—good or bad—Maddie would somehow be affected. There was no way to get around that.

Realizing Matthias was waiting for her answer, she cleared her throat and shook her head. "No, this assignment isn't becoming too much for me. I guess I just have to...not care so much?"

Matthias gave her a sad look and then walked over and sat down at one of the long tables. "Little angel, you do not have the ability to just decide not to care. It is not the way you were created. As for your present concern, little Sarah will recover in time to get the transplant. She is being tested even now."

Charity was overcome with gratitude and thankfulness and launched herself at Matthias, hugging him tightly before she released him and did a little somersault in the air even as her wings unfurled....

"Charity!" Matthias stern voice immediately dampened her celebration. She halted mid-turn and slowly lowered her feet back to the floor and folded her wings up once again.

"Sorry," she told him sheepishly. "I was just so..."

Matthias tried to hide his smile as he nodded. "I understand, but the rules..."

"...are there to protect us all." Charity looked chagrined and then her smile burst forth. "Thank you for telling me."

Matthias returned her smile and then tipped his head toward the door. "Choir practice is about to start."

Charity shook her head and headed for the door at a run. "I don't have time for that right now. I have a miracle to witness."

. . ⁓ . .

NICK LOOKED AT SARAH'S vitals one last time and then glanced at the clock above the door. If there was any way possible to justify her having the transplant, he intended to find it. Fever or not.

He'd told Maddie and Zach that he needed to sign a few papers and would be back shortly. He'd hoped the lab would have already sent someone up to the third floor, but it had been twenty minutes and he still hadn't seen anyone.

He picked up the phone and called downstairs again.

"Lab," someone answered.

"Yes, this is Dr. Stavros up on the third floor."

"Hello, doctor. Was there something else you needed?"

"I'm just wondering when your tech is going to be up here..."

"Dr. Stavros?" a voice called from the employee lounge doorway.

He glanced up and told the person on the other end of the line, "Never mind." He replaced the phone and then frowned. "Dr. Stansfield?"

She smiled as she came entered the room. "Oh, no need for formalities. There's no one else around right now."

Nick saved the file he was working on and shut the laptop. "I prefer to keep things professional. What are you doing up on the third floor? The last time I looked, we didn't have any microscopes or centrifuges lying around."

Julia looked like she wanted to take issue with his professional stance, but then she straightened her shoulders and lifted the small phlebotomy cart in her hand. "I understand you have a transplant patient up here who is running a fever? I came up to personally see if we can find the bug responsible and get things under control before that kidney touches down."

Nick nodded and then headed for the doorway. "Follow me. The patient is a seven-year old girl, recovering from a kidney tumor which resulted in removal of her left kidney. Unfortunately, during the surgery, it was discovered that the renal arteries were conjoined. An attempt was made to bisect them, however, the blood flow to her right kidney was seriously compromised. The chemotherapy further damaged her renal function and she entered renal failure six weeks ago. She was moved up to the top three on the transplant list last week."

"And just when a match is found, she spikes a fever," Julia surmised as they walked down the hallway together.

"That's about it. The family hasn't been told yet. I didn't want to worry them. Yet. They've been through so much..."

"Let's find out what's wrong and fix it then. She's got, what? Three or four hours?"

"The kidney will be here in less than two hours and we can keep it in cold preservation for twenty-four hours, maybe thirty-six."

Julia smiled encouragingly at him. "Plenty of time to get a handle on whatever is making your girl sick. Let's get some specimens."

"I'm going to take the family down the hallway while you do that." They entered Sarah's room where her entire family was sitting with her, smiles on their faces and hope in their eyes. "How are we doing, family?"

"Dr. Nick is Sarah really going to get a new kidney?" her Aunt Liza asked.

"That's the plan. Sarah, this is Dr. Stansfield. She's going to help me get some samples and such so that we can check off a few more boxes before the transplant surgery. Can I steal your mom and aunt for a few minutes?"

Sarah nodded. "When you come back, will you tell me about the surgery?"

Nick smiled at her. "Sure thing, my curious little patient. In fact, I bet I could have one of the nurses round up a book or video about it. I might even be able to get Dr. Mantlo up here."

"Who is Dr. Mantlo?" Sarah asked.

"The doctor who will be taking the lead during your surgery," Nick told her.

"He's one of the best," Julia added.

Sarah smiled and nodded. "I know. Dr. Nick would never let anybody else treat us."

Julia raised her brows and looked at Nick. "High praise coming from someone so young."

Nick chuckled and shared a look with Sarah. "She is not your average patient. Let me go talk to your mom and aunt. Dr. Stansfield just needs a few samples, and then she'll be out of here."

"Is she here because of my fever?" Sarah asked quietly, reaching out and grabbing his hand as he started to move away.

Nick paused and looked at her. "They told you?"

Sarah shook her head. "No. I was watching the computer screen. Besides, I could see the look on their faces. They were worried."

"Well, I don't want you to be," Nick informed her, tapping her lightly on the nose. "We've got this." He looked at Julia and nodded once before leaving the room. Sarah was a very bright little girl and almost too smart for her own good. He just hoped she hadn't shared her fears with her family members. Her mother wasn't as capable of dealing with bad news right now. She was understandably worried about her daughter and a whole slew of other concerns. Nick only hoped they would be able to keep worry about some sort of infection off her radar.

Chapter 23

"Maddie?" Zachary's soft voice caused her eyes to open halfway. She'd agreed to stay in the little boy's room while Nick looked in on Sarah and a few of his other patients. Her head had started pounding more insistently in the last hour and all she really wanted to do was find a soft bed in a dark room and end this day.

Seeing Zach watching her worriedly, she pushed herself to a more upright position and gave him a small smile. "What's up?"

"You were frowning in your sleep."

"I was? I didn't mean to," Maddie told him, lifting a hand to rub at her temple. She glanced at the large clock and then stood up. "Dr. Nick's been gone a while. I should go see what's keeping him."

"Do you have to go?" Zach asked.

"I don't have to," Maddie told him. She sat down next to his bed and asked, "Are you excited about seeing your grandmother for Christmas?"

Zach nodded. "Do I really get to leave the hospital?"

"That's what Dr. Nick said," Maddie reminded him.

"I know, but I still feel...weak?"

"Your body has been through a lot. Each day you'll feel a bit stronger."

Zach nodded and then he bit his bottom lip for a moment, clearly undecided about something. Maddie gave him plenty of time to decide if he was going to be brave enough to ask his question. She wasn't disappointed when he asked, "Can you help me?"

"With what?"

"Penny told me that, before I can leave the hospital, I have to be able to walk down the hallway. She tried to help me this morning, and..."

"And what?" Maddie asked quietly.

"I kind of gave up because it hurt."

"What hurt? Your legs?" Maddie asked, her nurse training pushing aside how she was feeling.

"I haven't walked for a while," Zach explained in his small voice.

"Ah. Well..." Maddie let the word drag out. "How about I rub your legs for a few minutes to get them awake and the blood moving and then we try again?"

"You'll help me?" Zach asked.

"Of course." Maddie folded back the sheet and then rubbed her hands together so that they wouldn't be cold. She then took his right leg and began to lightly massage the calf, including his foot, ankle and knee. She stopped one hand width above his knee and then moved to the left leg, repeating the same procedure.

"There, that should be enough to get the blood moving. Ready to give it a try?"

Zach looked uncertain but nodded anyway. "Okay. Where's Dr. Nick?"

Maddie shrugged her shoulders. "Down the hallway. Want me to go get him?"

"No! I mean...I don't want him to know if I can't do it. He might change his mind..."

"...about letting you come home for Christmas?" Maddie surmised.

Zach nodded. "I want to go live with Dr. Nick, even if it's only for a little while."

Maddie decided not to argue the time limit Zach was placing on his pending visit to Nick's house. Maddie knew without having it fully spelled out that Nick was hoping to make Zach a permanent resident of his home. For both of their sakes, Maddie was hoping that small miracle came true. It was the season for miracles, after all.

She'd not been one to hold much hope this last year for any sort of a future not filled with pain and misery, but something had changed in the last week. Suddenly, she didn't want to be at the cemetery. She wanted to be with other people. Zach. Her co-workers. Nick. She even had a small desire to see her mother and Miah's mom.

Deciding that now wasn't the time to try and figure it all out, Maddie gave Zach an encouraging smile and then reached for the non-slip socks lying on the side table. "Here, we need to keep those toes warm."

Once they were on and Zach had stuck his arms through a robe, Maddie held his upper torso while he slid his body off of the bed. Once his feet were on the floor, she held him up until she felt his legs straighten and his body quit wobbling. She leaned back and looked at his face. "Good?"

Zach nodded and then took a breath. "I'm good."

Maddie shifted so that she was standing beside him, his frail arm holding onto her waist as she wrapped an arm around his shoulders. With her other arm, she held the rolling IV cart, making sure the line didn't get tangled up or stepped on.

"I've got you. Let's try going to the doorway, shall we?"

Zach nodded and carefully placed one foot in front of the other. He relied heavily on her support the first few steps, but then he grew more confident and a bit stronger. By the time they reached the door, he was walking slowly on his own. "I did it."

"Yes, you sure did," Maddie hugged him lightly. "Now, let's go back to bed. That's enough for one night."

"Just a bit further. Please? My legs don't hurt now, and it feels really good to be out of bed."

"I bet it does," Maddie murmured. "Okay. Just a bit further. You've got plenty of time to practice your skills tomorrow."

She pushed the door open and then kept hold of Zach's shoulders as he slowly stepped out into the hallway. He stood there, looking up and down the hallway, a smile upon his pale face. "This is the first time I've been out of my room and not in a wheelchair or bed for weeks."

"This proves you're getting better," Maddie murmured.

"I want to leave here."

"And you will, but I think Dr. Nick wants you to get a bit stronger first. That means you need to eat and get plenty of sleep. Think you can make it to the window?" she nodded to her right.

Zach eyed the window and nodded. "That doesn't look too far."

Maddie inwardly applauded his confidence and held onto him as they made the short walk. Once there, Zach leaned heavily against the windowsill, looking out at the bright blue sky and the sun shining. It was easy to pretend it was just a happy summer day, until one glanced at the piles of snow on the ground below. Then, it looked cold and icy.

They stood there for several minutes before footsteps sounded behind them. Maddie turned her head to see Nick walking toward them, his head down and a look of worry on his face. She kept one hand on Zach and called Nick's name.

He blinked twice before a smile appeared. "Zach, I'm impressed."

"Thanks, Dr. Nick. Maddie helped me and I managed to walk out here." Zach wavered slightly.

"I think he's had enough," Maddie murmured to Nick, who nodded and immediately came to Zach's other side.

"Let's get you back to bed."

Zach took two steps and then almost fell over as exhaustion set it. Nick gave him a tender smile and then swept him up into his arms. He nodded at the IV pole, and Maddie nodded back. Together, they got the young boy settled back in bed. He was almost asleep by the time they finished tucking him back into bed and making sure his vitals were recorded.

"He looks so peaceful," Maddie murmured, absently rubbing her temple again.

Nick noticed almost immediately. "He's such a special little boy."

Maddie recalled the look of worry on his face. "Nick, what's happening with the others?"

"With Sarah?" When she nodded, he blew out his breath. "Let's get out of here."

Maddie nodded and allowed Nick to steer her from the room and down the hall to the lounge. She settled in a chair and closed her eyes for a moment.

"You're tired and hurting. I need to get you back home," Nick told her, handing her a bottle of water from the fridge in the corner.

"Thanks. My head hurts a little bit, that's all."

"You have a concussion. I'm thinking it might hurt more than a little bit."

Maddie shrugged. "Maybe. Anyway, tell me about Sarah."

Nick opened his mouth to begin when Dr. Stansfield, from the lab, came into the room. He straightened and took the papers she held out to him. "What did you find?"

"You'll be happy to know that your patient only has a slight urinary tract infection. I already ordered the proper antibiotics to clear it out. I've left orders for a follow-up test in twelve hours. She should be ready for surgery after that."

Maddie watched relief and hope fill Nick's face. "Julia...thank you. I know you had to have pulled some strings to get those results done so quickly."

Julia shrugged and then smiled coyly at him. "Thankful enough to get some dinner with me? You've been putting me off for months now."

Maddie was a little shocked when the beautiful doctor reached out and touched Nick's collar, straightening it before Nick moved backward. The fact that she was completely being ignored by the other doctor was also shocking. The other woman followed Nick's retreat, until he slid sideways and put Maddie between them.

Feeling like a third wheel, Maddie grabbed her purse and prepared to leave. "Excuse me..."

Nick gave her a look and then placed a hand on her shoulder, keeping her in place beside him. "Maddie, have you met Dr. Stansfield? She was kind enough to come up and personally take some samples from Sarah so that we could get ahead of the infection causing her fever."

Maddie nodded and then stuck out her hand. "I've seen you around the hospital. You work in the lab?"

"Head of Microbiology," the other woman replied, eyeing her carefully. "Did I interrupt something here? I thought this was the employee lounge?"

"It is. Maddie works up here."

Julia looked her up and down and then pulled a face. "I didn't realize anyone beside medical staff were allowed to utilize the lounge areas. Don't let word of that get around, I can promise you the surgical staff would not appreciate having the janitorial staff invading their lounges."

Nick cleared his throat before answering. "Maddie was in an accident and sustained a concussion. She's one of my nurses, and I've been looking after her."

"Well, that's very noble of you and taking your responsibilities as the head of pediatrics a little far, don't you think? I can't imagine what would happen if word was to get out."

"How I deal with my staff and run things on the third floor is, as you know, entirely up to me," Nick informed her tightly. "Furthermore, what I do on my personal time is...well...personal."

Julia's face dropped and Maddie watched as the woman tried to summon some remorse for her insinuations. "Nick...I didn't mean..."

He held up a hand to stop her. "I know exactly what you meant, as I'm sure Maddie would have if she wasn't under the weather. In fact, she's got a headache and we were just about to get out of here. Thank you for getting results for Sarah so quickly."

"Nick...Dr. Stavros..."

Julia looked confused when he took Maddie's elbow and led her from the lounge. He led her toward the elevators and told the nurses at the middle station that he'd check in later in the afternoon. As the elevator doors closed, Maddie glanced up to see a very irritated Julia Stansfield standing with her hands on her hips and a calculating look in her eyes.

The beautiful doctor wasn't used to being turned down, and unless Maddie had misread the signals she had been sending Nick, Dr. Julia Stansfield wasn't ready to quit pursuing the most eligible bachelor in Great Falls. Maddie wasn't sure for whom to feel more sorry. Nick had inadvertently made sure the woman would be upping her game to attach herself to him romantically. And Julia had just tipped her hand by showing how spiteful and judgmental she could be.

Maddie hadn't known Nick long, but she did know that he was the most genuine and humble man she'd ever met. He would have nothing in common with a woman like Julia. The sooner the woman figured that out, the better. As for Maddie, she was just coming to terms with losing Miah, so how was it possible that she was even considering the fact that she and Nick might have something beyond friendship in their futures?

After their kiss, she looked at him through a different lens. He'd given her fair warning that he thought they had something beyond friendship in their future, but she hadn't really wanted to believe it was possible. Then he'd kissed her, and her entire view of their relationship had changed. She could easily see herself falling for the handsome doctor, but she had so much baggage yet to get rid of, it just didn't seem fair to burden him with it.

On the ride back to Nick's house, she finally gave into the tiredness that pulled at her eyelids and let them close. Her headache was a constant throbbing now and her mind was a jumble of emotions and thoughts. *Just let them go for now. Everything will seem better after a nap.*

Chapter 24

Charity watched as Nick gently woke Maddie up and helped her back into his home. He helped her to the couch, retrieved a pain pill for her, and then insisted on her finishing the nap. Once Maddie gave in and closed her eyes, he stood in the doorway, watching her for the longest time with a contemplative look on his face.

After several minutes, Nick retreated to his home office and began going through his patients' charts again. The ones that were doing well brought a satisfied smile to his face. The ones that weren't showing good progress brought frown lines to his brow and prompted more research on the computer.

Charity wandered back into the living room where Maddie was beginning to wake up and watched from the corner. The young woman gingerly sat up, almost as if she were expecting to feel pain. As she rolled her shoulders and neck, rubbing the stiffness from the muscles there, a light smile came to her face. Charity knew she was going to make a full recovery.

Maddie looked around and called out, "Nick?"

When he didn't immediately answer her, she reached for her phone and glanced at the time. She scrolled through the screens before putting the phone away as she stood. She headed for the kitchen, almost colliding with Nick when he stepped out of his office unaware that she was awake.

"Whoa!" he caught her by the shoulders. "I didn't know you woke up."

"Just now."

"How's the head?" He squatted down and peered into her eyes for a moment.

"It's better," Maddie smiled. "Even my neck's not as sore."

"Good. Your eyes look better, too. Hungry?"

"A bit. Is Sarah really going to be alright and get the transplant?" Maddie asked as she followed Nick into the kitchen and sat down on a bar stool.

"Yes." Nick smiled as he pulled eggs and vegetables from the fridge. "Omelet sound good?"

"Really good," Maddie told him. Charity watched as Nick expertly cut up vegetables and added them to a hot skillet. Maddie seemed content to watch him as well and Charity tapped into her emotions, pleased with what she picked up. Maddie was developing feelings for the handsome doctor.

"Little angel, please tell me you're not interfering," Matthias' stern voice came from behind Charity.

She gasped and spun around, shaking her head. "No. I was just kind of...well, eavesdropping on her feelings. I didn't alter them or influence them or—"

"I know," Matthias said and smiled. "I was just checking. I wanted to give you a heads up. The little girl who went home for Christmas will be home for good before morning."

Charity's face fell and she turned and watched the interplay between Nick and Maddie. They were talking about the preparations Nick needed to take care of in order to make his home a proper place for Zachary and his grandmother for Christmas.

"I haven't even thought about getting the tree out of the garage. Guess I should probably take care of that tonight."

"I can help," Maddie offered.

Nick smiled at her. It broke Charity's heart to know that the peacefulness they were enjoying right now was about to come to an end.

• • ⁂ • •

THE PHONE RANG AND Nick slid the pan off the burner as he reached for it.

"Hello?"

"Dr. Stavros?" A hesitant voice came across the line.

Nick nodded and turned away from Maddie. "Yes. Who is this?"

"This is Brian...Paula's father," the man's voice broke before he could finish his sentence.

"Brian, is Paula—"

"She's still alive, but the hospice nurse said she's very close. I just wanted...we just wanted...to thank you."

Tears filled Nick's eyes, and he forced them back. "I'm headed your way right now."

"Thank you."

Nick hung up the phone and then dropped his head as he closed his eyes and let his tears fall. When he felt a small hand on his shoulder, he turned and found himself wrapped in Maddie's arms. He hugged her back and whispered brokenly, "She's almost finished with her race."

After a long pause, he sniffed and stepped away. "Thanks. I need to go—"

"Let me come with you. I only cared for her a handful of times, but I'd like to be there to offer...whatever help I can," Maddie told him in a soft whisper.

He nodded. After grabbing his keys off the hook by the garage door, he slipped his shoes on while she retrieved hers from the living room. When he noticed she didn't have her coat, he grabbed the extra one he kept by the door and held it while she slipped her arms inside.

The ride to Paula's home was completed in silence, with Maddie holding his hand the entire way. The hospice nurse met them at the front door and gave Nick a quick rundown on Paula's failing systems. "I'm sorry, Dr. Stavros."

"Is she comfortable?"

The hospice nurse nodded. "She's had little to no pain these last few hours as her breathing and such slowed down."

Nick nodded and then followed the nurse toward the family room at the back of the house. A hospital bed sat in the center of the room, facing the large stone fireplace and large Christmas tree with multi-colored lights twinkling brightly.

Brian met them and, after shaking Nick's hand, he turned to Maddie who hugged him before going over and doing the same to his wife. Little Tommy was curled up in a chair next to his sister, looking at a picture book and telling Paula all about the pictures since the words were too many and too long for him to read.

"Thank you for coming," Brian told him.

Nick came to stand beside Maddie. "Chelsea, I'm so sorry."

Paula's mother got up and hugged him. "Thank you for helping us give her one last Christmas. I don't know how you and your team pulled it off, but we'll always remember the time we had together."

"I wish I could have given you more time."

"We all wish that," Maddie added.

"What can we do to help?" Nick asked, feeling the need to do something.

"Just sit with us. Paula loved being at the hospital and under your care. Even when she was having one of her bad days, she found something to take her mind off of her pain and put a smile on her face. Thank you for that."

The words were heartfelt, and Nick acknowledged them as he always did, humbly and as a challenge to do better for the next child. No parent should ever have to suffer the way these parents were currently suffering. Children were supposed to bury their parents, not the other way around.

Dear God, please be with this family right now. Give them the assurance that Paula won't suffer any more once she's with you. I pray that their memories of the bad days will fade, and they'll only remember the good times they had with their daughter and sister.

Nick sat down next to Maddie and did his best to make small talk with Paula's parents while her body continued to shut down. After they'd been there for a while, Paula roused and opened her eyes. She smiled at him, and it was all Nick could do to smile back when inside his heart was breaking.

Paula reached weakly for Maddie's hand and then whispered, "Be happy. Dr. Nick is special."

Nick watched emotion clog Maddie's throat as she kissed the little girl on the forehead and promised to do so. "I know."

When she retreated to a chair at the end of the bed, he joined her, holding her hand and silently praying. Not for a miracle of healing, although Nick knew God was capable. Instead, he prayed for this journey to end sooner rather than later.

The hospice nurse was standing by to administer one final dose of Morphine that would allow Paula to go to sleep one last time and pass peacefully into eternity. Comfort care. That's what the hospice world called it, but in Nick's opinion, there was little comfort to be gained from watching your child die.

Two hours later, Paula's heart began to beat erratically, and her breathing became shallow and infrequent. Fifteen minutes later, she took her last breath and her heartbeat stopped. She passed into the arms of heaven while her parents sobbed in one another's arms. Little Tommy had fallen asleep on Maddie's lap. Nick watched as Maddie shed silent tears and cuddled the sleeping child who had just lost his only sibling.

Their lives would never be the same, and somehow Nick knew that he and Maddie's lives would be forever intertwined after having shared this experience.

Chapter 25

The next afternoon...

Maddie thanked the taxi driver and then smiled at George as he pushed open the hospital doors. "Good afternoon."

"The same to you. I thought Dr. Nick said you were taking the entire day off?" George asked, as he walked with her to the bank of elevators.

"I was going to, but Teresa called because Ciera went home not feeling well. I told her I was fine to come in and finish up her shift."

"Are you sure? You bumped your head pretty hard," George told her, pushing the button to call the elevator.

"I'm sure. Thanks for your concern," Maddie told him with a smile. The elevator doors opened and she stepped inside. "See you in a few hours."

"I'll be here. Can I give you a ride home? I noticed you took a taxi in."

"My car's still in the shop and won't be ready until next week sometime. After Christmas."

"Well, I'd be happy to give you a ride home."

"And I'd be happy to accept," Maddie told him as the doors closed.

Her smiled faded once she was alone. After leaving Paula's house the night before, she'd gotten almost no sleep. Neither had Nick. Instead, they'd stayed up talking about anything and everything. It had been very therapeutic in a way, and looking back, it was something she wished someone had forced her to participate in after Miah's death.

Instead, everyone had walked around her on eggshells, afraid to mention his name or anything of a personal nature for fear she would fall apart. They hadn't been wrong. She would have most definitely fallen apart, but looking back now, that would have been preferable to the self-imposed prison she'd lived in these last twelve-and-a-half months.

Nick had helped her see that grieving was a natural God-given way for humans to deal with their emotions and to properly categorize everything. By refusing to go through the process of grieving Miah's death, she'd robbed herself of the ability to move on and remember him fondly.

The elevator came to a stop, and the doors opened to a third-floor brimming with Christmas spirit. The elves had been busy decorating with paper chains of red and green, metallic glitter tinsel, and handmade snowflakes on white sparkly paper.

Maddie felt her spirits lighten as she made her way toward the nurses' desk and the children's smiles were infectious. She nodded at Marci who was just headed back down to answer a room call. "Hey, sounds like Christmas around here."

"Yeah, but we've had plenty of catastrophes today. Thanks for coming in to help out."

"No worries," Maddie assured her.

"I heard you were with Paula when she passed," Marci murmured.

Maddie felt tears fill her eyes as she nodded. "Yes. She's at peace now." She cleared her throat and then blinked her tears away. She and Nick had shared plenty of those the night before and had fallen asleep sitting on the couch with her head on his chest and his arms around her. They'd needed the comfort of knowing they weren't alone last night.

In the bright light of day, she'd silently wandered what it would have been like if she had allowed someone to be there for her on the day that she had received the news that Miah had been killed. She'd not allowed anyone to comfort her. Not his mother. Not her own. She'd retreated to her bedroom and huddled on her bed in a fetal position, refusing to acknowledge everyone who tried to reach out to her. It had been a mistake. One she didn't intend to repeat.

She gave Marci a half smile and then headed for the lounge to quickly change into another set of ridiculous scrubs. These were the pink ones with scenes from *The Nutcracker* depicted on them. As she stepped back out into the hallway, she hoped she didn't look as ridiculous as she felt. Penny was just returning to the nurses' station so Maddie joined her.

"So, what can I do to help?"

Penny looked her over and asked, "Are you sure you should be back to work already? After yesterday—"

"I feel okay." Maddie didn't mention the faint dizziness she'd experienced when she'd been getting out of the taxi. Nor did she mention the tiny bit of nausea that was still making itself known. She knew both symptoms probably meant she was suffering some after-effects of her concussion, but she hated sitting around doing nothing. She needed to keep busy or her mind would start spinning.

"So, why don't you start with Zach and work your way down that wing. I'll start at the other end and hopefully we'll meet in the middle."

"Sounds good. Any idea where Dr. Stavros is?" Maddie asked as she clocked in.

"One of his patients had a bad reaction to his chemo treatment this morning. Teresa went down to help."

Maddie nodded and, without another word, she headed for Zach's room. He was sleeping peacefully, so she quickly noted his vitals in the computer and then set an alarm to come back in thirty minutes and check on him again. His color looked a bit better today. She hoped that was something she'd be able to continue saying in the days and weeks to come.

She made her rounds before stopping at Sarah's room. Her aunt was working a crossword puzzle on the small couch, and her mother was knitting in the rocking chair. Sarah was also sleeping so Maddie gestured for Carol to join her in the hallway.

"Hi. How are things going?" Maddie asked.

Carol smiled brightly. "They're going to do the transplant first thing in the morning. The doctor has already been by to see Sarah and the last test from the laboratory came back clean. Her fever is completely gone, as well."

"That's wonderful news. Well, I'll be praying for a quick recovery for her and for the doctor's hands to be steady and true tomorrow."

"Thank you."

Maddie continued checking in on each patient. When her alarm went off thirty minutes later, she headed back to Zach's room. There were only a few rooms left for her to check on, but Teresa met her and offered to finish them for her.

"Thanks. I'm headed back to Zach's room to check on him. He was sleeping when I was there earlier."

"Okay. Dr. Stavros said he'd be up to see him after he finished his rounds."

Maddie nodded, hoping Nick wouldn't be too upset when he discovered that she'd come into work. He'd thought she was going to stay home and take it easy for the rest of the day. Not willing to dwell on that unhappy thought, she smiled and headed for the room at the end of the hall.

Zach was awake this time and she grinned at him as she entered. "There's the little man I was hoping to see."

"Maddie! Are you feeling better?"

"Much. How about you? Did you go for another walk today?"

Zach shook his head. "No. Could we take one now?"

Maddie grabbed her stethoscope from around her neck. "Let's get some vitals and then we'll discuss is."

"Okay."

She took his blood pressure and temperature, noting the slight elevation in the computer. "Okay, you ready for that walk?"

Lord don't let me get dizzy and cause him to fall. Those are headlines I really can do without enacting.

"First things first. Slipper socks and robe."

"I can put them on," Zach told her. She handed him one sock and watched as he pulled his foot up and after a few tries managed to get the sock in place.

"Want me to help with the second one?" she offered.

Zach shook his head. "No, I can do it. The more things I can do for myself, the faster I'll get strong enough to get out of here."

It was December twentieth and his grandmother was due to arrive late tomorrow. There was a huge snowstorm forecast so her chances of arriving on time were looking slim. Nick had sent the tickets for Clara to her daughter, Sheila, early this morning. Given the weather forecast, he'd included a round trip ticket for Sheila to accompany her mother all the way to Great Falls.

They were due to arrive around six o'clock tomorrow evening and, with Paula's passing, his house still wasn't ready. Maddie had agreed to help him get his tree set up this evening. She only hoped she still had enough energy to do so after working the next few hours.

"Ready to go?" Maddie asked, giving Zach her arm as he slid his feet over the side of the bed. She grabbed his IV pole and moved it to her left side, then lowered the bed all the way down. Once his feet were touching the tiled floor, she placed an arm around his shoulders and allowed him to scoot off the bed and stand up.

His legs were much stronger today, and he needed little help as they slowly walked from his room. There was music coming from the common room. He looked at her with wide eyes. "Can we go down there?"

Maddie gauged the distance, knowing it was much too far for him to walk there and back under his own steam. She pursed her lips and then met his eyes again. "I'll make you a deal. You can walk down there, but you have to ride back."

"Maybe I could walk both ways," Zach offered instead.

"I think that might be pushing it a bit too much. I could leave a note for the night nurses to let you take another walk before bedtime, though."

Zach considered her offer and then grinned. "Deal."

Maddie smiled and walked beside him, her arm around his back just in case he started to wobble. Zach did an amazing job, managing to walk the entire way and only becoming slightly out of breath. He'd been in bed for months. Any hopes he had of playing sports this year were going to be hinged on him getting constant exercise. She made a mental note to mention it to Nick this evening.

She led Zach over to a table with an empty seat and parked his IV pole behind him. "Hey, I'm going to leave you to get acquainted with some new friends for a few minutes. I'll be right back."

"That's okay," Zach whispered. "I like this movie. Can I stay and watch the rest of it?"

She glanced at the screen and couldn't help but laugh and shake her head. *Elf* was playing. "Sure. Enjoy and I'll be close if you need me."

"Thanks Maddie," Zach told her, pulling her arm and then hugging her tightly for a minute before joining in with his new friends.

Chapter 26

Maddie retreated to the nurses' station to find Dr. Nick watching her with a confounded expression. She met his eyes and decided she might as well find out if he was upset with her sooner than later.

"Hey."

"Hey?" he asked with an arch of his brow.

He glanced at the other ladies avidly listening to their exchange and then took her elbow and led her down the hall a few dozen feet. Maddie went with him willingly, not wanting whatever he had to say to her to be overheard.

"I thought I dropped you off at your apartment and you were going to rest this afternoon?" he asked, crossing his arms over his chest.

"I was, but then Ciera went home, and Teresa went down to the treatment rooms to help out. Penny was short-staffed and needed my help for a few hours."

Nick peered at her eyes and then scanned her face. "No headache?"

"Nothing I can't handle for a few hours. Besides, if I hadn't come in, Zach wouldn't have gotten to walk down the hallway and make some new friends."

Her statement got Nick's attention. "Zach walked down here?"

"I had my arm around his back the entire time, but...yes. I made him a deal that he could walk down but he had to ride back."

"That's...amazing. I'd like to discharge him tomorrow, but I'm thinking it might be better to get Clara settled and bring Zach home the day after."

"That might be better for both of them. It will also give Zach another full day to rest up and get some of his energy back." She glanced at Zach and frowned when she saw him leaning his chin heavily on his hand. "He's tired. I should..."

"...let him finish the movie. If he falls asleep at the table, he won't have been the only one. Half of those kids will have to be woken up or wheeled back to their rooms when the movie ends."

Maddie nodded and then turned to look at Zach, but a wave of dizziness caught her by surprise. She reached out blindly for the wall, hoping to keep herself from falling down.

"Whoa!" Nick caught her by the arms. "What just happened?"

Maddie swallowed for a moment and blinked, willing her blurred vision and dizziness to clear and the accompanying nausea to fade. After several long seconds and hearing Nick call her name several more times, she looked up at him and found her voice. "Sorry, I guess I just turned too fast."

"You got dizzy and turned a delightful color of pale green," he told her, lowering her into the wheelchair that had magically appeared courtesy of Marci. "Thanks."

Maddie shook her head even as she sank into the wheelchair's leather cushion. "I don't need this—"

"Yes, you do. Doctor's orders." Nick looked down the hallway and gestured for Penny. "Mark her off. She's going back home."

"What happened?" Penny asked concerned.

"I just turned too fast and got a bit dizzy—"

"And she looked like she was about to toss her cookies. She's going home under concussion protocol. Mark her off until after the holidays..."

"No! Nick...Dr. Stavros! I can't take a week off."

Nick completely ignored her. "Zach's watching the movie. Maddie's going to say her goodbyes. Have someone wheel him back to his room once it's over. He walked down here."

"What? That's awesome. I'll personally make sure he gets back to bed. I saw orders for labs to be drawn first thing in the morning."

Nick nodded, and Maddie listened in, waiting for a chance to argue with him about her forced time off.

"If his labs come back good, I'll discharge him the day after. Make sure he gets a chance to exercise those legs three or four times a day. I need him as strong as possible."

Penny nodded and then turned to Maddie. "Concussions are nothing to play around with. Follow the doctor's orders and we'll see you after Christmas."

"Wait...Penny..." Maddie said, but the nurse wandered off. Maddie turned to Nick. "I can't just take a week off. We'll be short-staffed."

"We'll be fine. I wrote orders for half a dozen patients to go home tomorrow morning and another five the day after. It's Christmas and chemotherapy and radiation treatments can wait forty-eight hours to begin again. Having a chance to be with their families and have a brief taste of normality is just as important to their recovery as the chemicals we'll pump into the bodies over the next several weeks."

Maddie wanted to argue with him, but she couldn't. He was right. It was Christmas and letting these children and their families experience that outside the hospital walls was a priceless gift. Even for those who wouldn't have their children with them this same time next year. Memories would be made over the next several days.

Please, God...Let there be enough staff to help when things get really rough. What I wouldn't have given for one last Christmas with Miah.

Instead of the searing pain that used to come with remembering Miah, she only felt sadness for a life lost too soon. The fact that she wasn't sobbing in tears as she remembered the last Christmas before he deployed was strange for her. Maddie felt Nick watching her, and when she didn't speak, he left her sitting in the hallway. She watched him tell Zach goodbye.

Maddie recalled telling Miah goodbye. At the airport. He'd looked so young in his uniform, but then again, all of the men in his group had looked the same. She didn't know how many of them hadn't returned. Not enough, she was sure.

"Maddie?" Nick squatted down in front of her wheelchair. "I'm sorry, but you know I'm right."

She glanced at him and sighed. "Yeah. I just...I hate being sick."

"Said every healthcare worker on the planet. We make the worst patients but look at the bright side. I need help getting ready for Christmas. Now, you can help me without worrying about work or getting too tired."

Maddie shrugged as he wheeled her into the elevator. "Was Zach upset that I was leaving?"

"A little bit, but I assured him that he was going to be seeing a lot of you."

"Why would you tell him that?" she demanded quietly as the elevator stopped at the second floor and several people stepped on.

Nick crouched behind her chair and whispered, "Because there's no way I'm letting you go home, alone. Not with the dizziness I just observed. How many times?"

Maddie stayed quiet as the elevator reached the ground floor and everyone began to file out. She knew what Nick was asking, but she didn't want to hear him lecture her about ignoring her own declining health. As he pushed her out of the elevator, she mentally groaned when George saw her and wandered over.

"What happened?" he demanded to know.

"She got dizzy and experienced some nausea. I'm guessing, by her silence, that this wasn't the first episode. I'm taking her home with me, and she's got the next week off."

George nodded in agreement and then gave her a stern look. "Follow doctor's orders, Maddie."

"I wish everyone would quit telling me that," she groused.

Nick and George chuckled as Nick pushed her toward the exit. George called after them, "Make sure she gets plenty of rest."

"Will do," Nick agreed as he wheeled her toward the parking garage. "Hear that? You're supposed to be a good patient and listen to me."

"There's really no need for this. If you'll just take me home..."

She trailed off when Nick stopped and came around her chair to kneel and look at her. She had no choice but to meet his eyes.

"Can you honestly tell me you would rather spend the next week alone, ignoring Christmas and suffering from whatever ill effects the concussion has left behind?"

After a long moment of watching him, she shook her head. "No, but you have things to do..."

"And I could really use your help. We'll be helping one another out." He gave her a charming smile and then added, "Besides, you've heard all about my childhood, and I know almost nothing about yours. I need extortion material, so you need to start spilling it."

"I never agreed to that," Maddie told him.

"Well, not in words, but you didn't try to stop me when I was telling you all of my embarrassing moments."

Maddie finally nodded. "Fine."

Nick smiled at her and kissed her briefly. "This is going to be fun."

Maddie rolled her eyes but shared a grin with him. He then slipped around and started the wheelchair moving once again, whistling a Christmas tune. Maddie couldn't contain her own excitement. By the time they were headed toward his house, she looked forward to the next few days.

Chapter 27

Late afternoon the next day...

"Maddie?" Nick asked as he walked into his house and tossed his keys on the hook by the garage door. He stepped into the kitchen and stopped and sniffed. Gingerbread. He walked over and peered into the lit oven and then looked around his home. The open concept design gave him a clear line of sight through the dining room and family living area.

The large tree he'd pulled from the garage the night before stood next to the hearth, the twinkling lights and delicate glass ornaments shimmering in welcome. Stockings he didn't even know he had were hanging from the mantle, and an elegant centerpiece sat in the middle of his dining room table.

"Maddie?" Nick called again, wandering through his home and recognizing that it truly felt like a *home*. Not just a house he came to at the end of each day.

"Your back," Maddie's voice came from the doorway of the guest room.

"The house looks amazing." He went to her and wrapped her in a welcoming hug. "I can't believe you did all of this. And the cookies in the oven..."

Maddie smiled and nodded. "My mom always baked gingerbread during the holidays. I guess it's one of those traditions I've claimed as my own."

"Well, it's a good one." Nick looked around once more and then glanced at the watch on his wrist. "I guess I should head for the airport. Sheila and Clara should be landing within the hour. You'll come with me?"

Maddie looked confused and then shook her head. "I..."

"Please? Maddie, these last few days..." Nick looked at her and then sighed. "I have no idea what's going on between us."

Maddie shook her head. He reached out and touched her shoulder, halting her movements. He gazed at her, struggling to make sense of the feelings she evoked inside of him. She wasn't just a member of his staff at the hospital. She'd become...more.

Last night, after setting up the Christmas tree, he'd gotten her to talk about her childhood. She'd talked about Miah being something from her past while shedding a few tears. Nick had listened, and afterward, he'd lightened the mood with stories from med school. He had her laughing before long and it had done both of them good.

The week had been hard. Not only because of her accident, but there had also been as much bad news as good this week, and it wasn't over yet. Nick was tired. For the first time that he could remember, he wasn't sure he could handle any more bad news.

"What's wrong?" Maddie asked, walking a bit closer to him.

He gave her a wry smile and then shook his head. "It's just been a week."

"I agree with that. How did Sarah's surgery go?"

Nick smiled. This was one of the bright spots of his week. "Good. Very good. All of the initial tests indicate it will be a successful transplant and if everything goes well, she'll get to go home shortly after the New Year begins."

"That's wonderful news. So, why do you look so...I don't know...down?"

"Hazards of the job. Anyway, I don't want to think about that right now. Let's head for the airport...." His phone rang and he pulled it from his pocket and answered it, concerned when he saw Sheila's number on the screen.

"Sheila?"

"Nick. Yes, it's me. We made it to Denver just fine, but they've been getting snow, off and on, all day and they just grounded all departing flights until tomorrow."

"What? That's...well, that's horrible. What are they doing to accommodate you?"

"I was lucky enough to secure a room for mom and me at one of the airport hotels. We're waiting for the shuttle right now."

"And Clara? How is she handling everything?"

"She's tired. There's no way she could have made this journey by herself. In unfamiliar surroundings, she doesn't even seem to have the basic skills to fend for herself."

Nick nodded and then walked into the family room, gesturing for Maddie to join him. "Unfortunately, many elderly suffering from one of the dementia diseases exhibit similar symptoms. Didn't the doctors treating her warn you of this?"

"They did, I guess she's just been coping better in the house."

"She would. Everything there is familiar to her, both in the present and in the past. I'm sorry I asked her to come out here. My intention wasn't to cause her distress."

"I know that."

"So, have they told you when the flight will be rescheduled yet?"

"No. They won't tell us anything until eight o'clock tomorrow morning. I'll call you then and let you know what the new plan is."

"Okay. Do I need to speak with Clara?"

"Frankly, she's very disoriented right now and I think it might be better for everyone if I just get her to the hotel, get her fed, and let her sleep for the night."

"I'll trust your judgment on that. Talk to you in the morning and please call if you need anything. Not sure how much help I can be long distance, but I'll do whatever I can to make your stay as comfortable as possible."

"Thank you. The airlines are actually being very accommodating and there comes our shuttle now. I'll talk to you in the morning."

"Goodnight." He disconnected the call and then place the phone on the coffee table. "Well, as you probably surmised, they ran into weather in Denver and the flights have been delayed until much later."

"So, they'll be here tomorrow?"

"That's right. Sheila said Clara was disoriented...maybe asking her to come out here was a bad idea." Nick needed to get her signature on the paperwork to transfer guardianship of Zachary to him, but not at the risk of her own health.

He scrubbed a hand over his jaw and then took a deep breath. "So...since our plans for the evening have tanked, how about I take us out to dinner?"

Maddie looked uncertain and then offered, "I could make something here?"

"No, you've done enough. As soon as your cookies..."

"Oh no!" Maddie spun around and darted back into the kitchen. She pulled the cookies from the oven and set the pans on the stove top. "Thank goodness. I almost burned them."

Nick followed her, watching her move around the kitchen to slide the cookies from the hot pan to the cooling racks. *Cooling racks? Where did those come from?*

Maddie looked up and then chuckled. "You look confused."

"I am. Did I have cookie sheets and cooling racks hiding in my kitchen?" Nick asked.

Maddie's laugh grew. "No. When I went back to my apartment to get some clothing, I grabbed a few extra things."

"Ah. That explains it. So, about dinner?"

"Ok. But I really could cook something here," she offered again.

"Let's have someone else do the cooking and cleanup. How does Italian sound?"

"Fattening, but good," Maddie replied. "Let me just grab my coat."

Nick watched her head back for the guest room and then snagged a cookie. He bit into it, and his eyes closed.

"These are wonderful," he called out.

She returned, putting her arms into her coat. "Glad you like them. I was thinking...maybe the kids on the floor would like to decorate gingerbread men?"

"I'm sure they would, but you're supposed to be taking it easy. Speaking of which, how's the dizziness?" He opened the garage door and helped her into the vehicle.

"It comes and goes," Maddie told him as he slid behind the driver's seat.

"Well, I'm scheduled to have the day off tomorrow so you can take it easy and we'll see if we can get them to disappear altogether."

"If only it was that easy," Maddie murmured.

Nick drove them out of the garage and toward his favorite restaurant. Gino was taking control of the front and greeted him with a warm smile. "Doc! It's great to see you again."

"Thanks, Gino. How's Amelia?"

"Doing great thanks to you."

"Glad to hear it. This is Maddie Jacobs. She's one of the new nurses on the third floor."

Gino smiled, telling her, "Best hospital floor in the country and best doctor around. Come this way, and I'll get you kids set up."

Maddie followed Gino. They were seated at a semi-private table near the back. The red and black décor, combined with the smells of roasted garlic, tomatoes, and basil had Nick's mouth watering in no time.

"Special's lasagna, or I can bring you some menus," Gino offered as he poured two glasses of water from a nearby pitcher.

"Lasagna sounds wonderful," Maddie told him with a smile.

"I concur."

"Be back in a jiffy with it." Gino smiled at them once again and disappeared toward the kitchens.

"On a first name basis with restaurant owners." Maddie smiled. "I'm impressed."

"Gino's daughter Amelia had leukemia a few years ago. With a successful bone marrow transplant, she's fully recovered."

"Another Dr. Stavros success story."

"I don't act alone. So, I was thinking...the house looks wonderful, but I noticed there's nothing to put beneath the tree."

Maddie smiled and then blushed. "Uhm...I might have done a little shopping online."

"You did?" Nick asked.

"Well, I just thought that maybe Zach needed a few toys and some clothing..."

"I agree. Maybe you could show me what you've already purchased, and I could add to it? I also need to get a few things for Clara."

"I can help you when we get home," Maddie offered.

Nick was glad the weather had delayed Clara's arrival. It gave him more time with Maddie; time he was really looking forward to.

Chapter 28

Maddie was enjoying herself in a way she hadn't done in a long time. After Nick had left for work that morning, she'd hailed a taxi and gone back to her own apartment. It had seemed lonely. She'd gathered clothing, makeup, and a few personal items. She'd also gathered a few things that she thought Zachary might enjoy, including some baking supplies and kitchen items she wasn't sure Nick would have. She'd not been wrong.

When she'd gotten back to Nick's home, she'd gone through the last of his Christmas storage boxes and then she'd pulled out her laptop and ordered a few things for Zachary. A new baseball mitt, a tee-ball set, and a couple of board games she remembered enjoying when she was a little girl. She was excited to see Zach's face on Christmas morning.

"What's that little smile on your face about?" Nick asked as they drove back to his home.

"Just thinking that today was a good day. I…I didn't even think about going to the cemetery. That's kind of a big step for me."

"And why is that?" Nick asked.

Maddie held her response until Nick pulled into the garage and they had entered the house. She walked toward the lit tree and settled in the corner of the couch. When Nick joined her a few minutes later, she tried to give voice to her thoughts.

"Since the funeral, I've been in a fog. After a few weeks, the only place I could really feel grounded was the cemetery. I would stay there for hours sometimes, talking to Miah about all of the plans we had for the future. Then I would remember that there was going to be no future, which would bring on lots of tears. I really only had my work at the hospital and my visits to the cemetery. I cut off everyone else. No friends from work. I ignored Miah's mom. I had more meaningful conversations with George at security than anyone else in my life."

"If you were telling me that this had only lasted for a few weeks to a few months, I'd say it might be a normal response to losing someone who meant so much to you."

"Maybe, but it just became a...routine. And then it became easier to pretend the funeral and such hadn't been reality. That Miah was going to come home one day, but deep down, I always knew that wasn't true."

"And that brought about its own self-recriminations and guilt," Nick added for her.

"Yeah. But since coming onto the third floor, and then...spending time with Zachary and...you...I want more from life. I want to live again."

"I'm glad," Nick told her. "I'm really glad about that."

They shared a smile and then sat in silence, listening to the soft Christmas carols coming from the speaker in the corner by the tree and watching the fire Nick had lit a few moments earlier. Maddie felt at peace here. She didn't even want to think about how she was going to feel when the holidays were over, and she returned to her lonely apartment and her job. She would miss spending time with Nick, but she imagined she would miss spending time with Zachary even more. The little boy had gotten beneath her defenses and firmly inserted himself into her heart.

"Want to show me the things you have coming for Zachary? I have to admit, with everything else going on these last few days, I really hadn't given much thought to that. Or Christmas dinner."

"We can take care of dinner easily enough." Maddie pulled out her phone and activated a local big box store's app. "Just select what you need from the store and then the day and time you wish to pick it up."

"Really?" Nick asked, taking the phone from her hand. He scrolled through the screens for a moment and then looked up at her. "This is amazing."

"It's how to shop in these modern days. No need to spend an hour walking around the grocery store. You can stand in front of your fridge and pantry, select what and how many of each item you need, and then you pull up to the store at the selected day and time. It's loaded into the back for you by a friendly store employee."

"That's amazing. I will definitely be using this. So, help me put together a dinner menu."

Maddie chuckled and then joined him on the other couch when he patted the empty space by his side. "Okay, so...choose your protein."

"Turkey. That is, if you know how to cook one? I have to admit I've never tried. The last time my parents came for Christmas I ordered one of those pre-made, pre-cooked dinners from a local diner."

"I can cook a turkey and everything else we need for dinner," she assured him. As they selected the items needed and added in a few things for breakfasts and lunches, anyone watching them would have thought they were an established couple. The way they seemed to work together and shared the same likes and dislikes. Neither of them noticed, caught up in the moment as they were.

. . ⁌ . .

CHARITY SMILED AS SHE watched Maddie and Nick interact. She was still celebrating Maddie's own admission that she hadn't given a thought to visiting the cemetery all day long. It was a major breakthrough and seeing her enjoying time with Nick had Charity thinking that maybe what Maddie truly needed was sitting right beside her.

She did a little twirl as she exited the house and headed back up to the heavens. She'd missed the last choir practice. She was anxious to celebrate with her friends and hear about how their tasks were going. She'd been charged with helping Maddie let go of her sadness. She'd not really thought that would also include helping her love again. It seemed Christmas miracles were in bountiful supply.

She entered the choir room and then joined the choir head when he signaled her over.

"Yes, sir?"

"Charity, you exude joy right now."

"Thank you, tis the Season."

"Yes, but the last time I saw you, I thought you looked very worried."

"I might have been, but everything is working out splendidly with my charge."

"That's good to hear. I was hoping you might share some of your present joy by singing the opening solo section of today's piece?"

Charity smiled and nodded enthusiastically. "I would love to. Thank you."

"Well, get back in place and we'll begin. Everyone, please take your places and turn to page seventy-two."

Charity made her way to her place, noticing that neither Hope nor Joy had made practice today. She briefly lifted them up with a prayer for wisdom as they tried to help their charges. Then the angelic orchestra began, and she opened her mouth and began to sing out. She poured all of the joy she was feeling into the words, her face shining with the glory of the moment.

Sopra i cieli e ancor pi s (Angels we have heard on high)
Dolci canti gli angeli (Sweetly singing o'er the plains,)
E dai monti fin qua gi (And the mountains in reply)
Portan gioia ai deboli (Echoing their joyous strains.)

Gloria, in excelsis Deo!
Gloria, in excelsis Deo!

The Latin words rang out and, as they reached the Gloria section, the entire angelic chorus joined in, lifting their voices in exaltation of the most remarkable event in the history of the universe. Matthias watched from the courtyard as Charity sang her part to perfection. He was proud of the angel and based upon what he'd just observed on Earth, she was going to graduate easily in a few days. He looked forward to that day.

He waited until practice was over and then made sure Charity saw him standing in the middle of the courtyard. "Little angel, that was beautiful."

"Thank you," Charity answered him. "There's been an exciting new development."

"I saw," Matthias told her.

"You did?"

"I went to Earth to check on you and your friends and observed your charge and the good doctor having a fight with flour. Humans are very strange as I see nothing amusing about tossing handfuls of the white powder at one another, but they were giggling and then ended up kissing."

Charity giggled at the disgruntled look on Matthias' face. "Humans are indeed strange creatures. But that is just further proof of my great revelation. Maddie and Nick are falling in love."

"That is good news and will become very important in the coming days. Zachary is going to be brought home and it will take both of them to help him adjust to his new life."

"They are going to make such a lovely family."

Matthias smiled and nodded. "Yes, they are. Good job, Charity. Graduation is in three days. I look forward to announcing that fact to the rest of Heaven."

Charity laughed and let her wings unfurl. She rose up in the air and executed several somersaults before returning to the courtyard. Her wings folded against her back and she launched herself into her mentor's arms. "Thank you! This is indeed a day for celebration!"

Matthias looked uncomfortable being hugged, but Charity didn't care. She headed back down to Earth to watch and bask in the love story being written moment by moment. Humans might be strange creatures at times, but the love they were capable of showing was something that only the Creator of Heaven and Earth could have devised. And that was a show worth watching.

Chapter 29

December twenty-third...

"He's finally asleep," Maddie told everyone currently gathered in the family room of Nick's home. After arriving in Great Falls the day before, Sheila had announced that she didn't feel it was a good idea to leave her mother there and wished to let her visit for a day and then escort her back home.

Nick had been disappointed, but after seeing Clara's mental state for himself, he was in complete agreement. He and Maddie had taken Sheila and Clara to the house and then he'd left to go retrieve Zachary from the hospital. Maddie had wanted to be there, but she had thought it was better to stay with the other two women and make sure the elderly grandmother was as comfortable as possible.

"That's good."

She settled on the couch next to Nick. When he reached for her hand, she gave it, knowing that the action wasn't missed by Zach's aunt. His grandmother had retired shortly after dinner, leaving the other three adults a chance to discuss the future now that Zachary was also retired for the night.

"Nick, I think it's best if I take Clara home first thing tomorrow morning. I checked with the airline, and there's a flight that leaves at eleven and changes planes only once in Denver."

"I understand. Tomorrow is Christmas Eve and your family expects you home. I can't thank you enough for making sure she had a chance to see Zachary again."

"I realize this is probably the last time she will get to do so," Sheila told them sadly. "My mother's days are numbered." She reached for some papers lying on the side table and slid them across the coffee table toward Nick. "Those should enable you to apply for legal guardianship of Zachary with the Montana Department of Child Services."

Nick looked at Maddie and then picked up the paperwork. He flipped through them and then shook his head. "I don't understand."

"After speaking to you, I contacted the attorney who handled Jeff's final affairs. At the time Jeff created his will, mom hadn't received her diagnosis yet. I asked him if Jeff had ever expressed a backup plan and he told me he had. It wasn't discussed during the reading of the will because mom was still keeping her condition a secret from everyone but a few close family members.

"If she had disclosed it, she would have never been named Zachary's guardian in the first place."

"But these papers state that I am Zachary's legal guardian," Nick asked her. "They're signed by the court and everything."

"They are completely legal. The attorney filed an emergency ruling due to the sensitive nature of this case. I am supposed to wish you a Merry Christmas and thank you for all you do to help heal children with cancer. The judge's own daughter suffered from a rare blood cancer when she was an infant. She sadly didn't survive, but he has a soft spot for children who find themselves dealing with the same horrid disease."

"The world seems very small all of a sudden," Nick murmured.

Sheila smiled and cleared her throat. "Those are our family's gift to you and to Zachary. He deserves to live a normal life in a family that loves and has plenty of time for him. I wasn't sure if that was going to be here, but after seeing you and Maddie and how much Zachary loves you both, I couldn't be more pleased to know that my nephew is going to be raised here in Montana."

Nick squeezed her hand and then stood up and met her as she did the same, coming together in a hug. Maddie felt tears sting her eyes as she followed suit and was engulfed in the woman's warm embrace.

Sheila wiped her eyes and then took a step back. "I hope you'll both consider coming to visit us in Louisiana. I would like Zachary to get to know his cousins before they are all grown."

"We'll see what we can do," Nick replied.

"Thank you. Goodnight."

Maddie watched Sheila head for the stairs and the guestroom she was currently using. When she turned back, she found Nick watching her with a smile on his face. "What?"

"You didn't take issue with anything Sheila said."

"I didn't," Maddie agreed. "Should I have?"

Nick took her hand and pulled her over to the large carpet in front of the fire. He sat down and then tugged on her hand until she did the same. "You do realize Sheila thinks you and I are a thing. In a relationship."

"Uhm..."

"I guess I was wondering what you thought about that," Nick asked as he moved a piece of stray hair behind her ear.

Maddie looked at the dancing flames of the fire. Over the last few days this place had started to feel like home. Having Zachary here only made it that much more real. "I guess...I'm not sure what to say."

"Do you like being here?" Nick asked.

"You know I do," she answered him. "But you have to think about Zachary now. And we've only known each other a short time."

"Those sound like excuses. When I think about Zachary, I know having you in his life is the right thing to do. As for the amount of time we've known one another, that's a non-issue. The way I see it, we have the rest of our lives to learn each other's secrets."

Maddie felt her heart race and she sat up and moved a few inches away from him. "What are you saying?"

"I'm saying that, when the time is right, I think we should make this little family unit official." Maddie opened her mouth to speak but he laid a finger over her lips. "I know it's too soon. You still need to work through some things regarding your late fiancé, and I need to figure out how to make things flow at work."

"I hadn't even considered the impact a relationship between us might have on the hospital. Fraternizing is..."

"Discouraged but not completely denied. I think I have a working solution, but I haven't gotten all of the details worked out yet. It would involve you transitioning from a strictly floor nurse to a transitional treatment and follow-up team member."

"What does that even mean?" Maddie told him. "Transitional treatment? Follow-up team member?"

Nick settled back on his elbow and explained, "I've often thought that our patients and their families could use some help as they transition back to their normal lives. Whether it's because they've gone into remission, had a successful surgery, or are just going home to spend their last earthly days surrounded by friends and family. Hospice is great, don't get me wrong, but we take these patients and their families into our own while they are with us. Then we send them home and hope for the best."

"That's true but most of them seem to do alright," Maddie told him.

"I want them to do more than just alright. I want them to feel like they have help and support as they transition home. No matter the end result. That means we need someone out there, visiting homes and apartments, who truly understands the atmosphere we've created on the third floor. I think you could be that person."

"Me? But I've just started working up on the third floor," Maddie told him. "Surely Penny or one of the other nurses would be a better fit?"

"I've spoken to them all about it and they all agree it's a great idea, but they have no interest in getting that involved in their patients' lives. I watched you at Paula's house and you offered silent support, you listened, and you helped without being asked in a way that wasn't intrusive and was just right for the situation. That's what I want."

"So, I wouldn't be on the floor any longer?"

"Part time only. You would still coordinate with Hospice as needed, but also with home health care providers and other community support agencies to see that our families get everything they need and more. What do you think?"

"It sounds like a dream position, but...what will everyone at the hospital think? I haven't exactly made a lot of friends this past year."

"You haven't made enemies either," Nick reminded her. "Many people knew something wasn't quite right, but you seemed to be needing space and they gave it to you. Right or wrong."

He paused and then asked, "I heard you speaking to your mother earlier."

"She called from the cruise ship to wish me a Merry Christmas."

"You sounded genuinely happy."

"I am. She said the same thing." Maddie looked at her hands for a minute and then told him, "I called Miah's mom again. We had a good talk and she asked if she could come visit in February. She said she has some of Miah's things she'd been keeping for me."

Nick was watching her, and she appreciated his silent support. "She's coming out February fourth."

"Good. She can use the guest room."

"I didn't mean she needed to stay here," Maddie informed him.

"About that...I was thinking...this is a big house, as you've seen. I have plenty of room and I was wondering if you would want to move in here and help me with Zachary. You could have your own room down here, until we're ready to move to the next step. There would be no pressure from me..."

"You're asking me to move in here?"

Nick nodded. "I need help with Zachary. I realize that after today and I want that person to be you."

"I want to help. I just don't want us to get in over our heads."

"I don't want that either. Move in as a friend for now and I'll keep trying to woo you with my boyish charms. I don't know if anyone told you, but I'm considered quite a catch around the hospital," Nick informed her with a wink.

Maddie chuckled, "I've heard. Dr. Stansfield seemed quite taken with you."

Nick groaned. "That woman comes close to stalking me. She's always turning up and issuing invitations to join her."

"She has good taste," Maddie told him.

"Really?" Nick asked.

"Sure. It's just a little misguided," Maddie told him. "It's directed at something she's never going to have."

Nick sighed and then hugged her close. "Thank, God. She gives me a bad feeling every time she corners me. You should help dissuade her from pursuing me any longer."

"And how do you propose I do that?" Maddie asked.

"By telling her you're my girlfriend. You can choose to add the fact that you're also my roommate, or not. I don't care, just as long as she leaves me alone from now on."

"Girlfriend?" Smiling, Maddie said the word. "It has a nice ring to it."

"When you're ready to make it more, there will definitely be a nice ring involved."

"One step at a time," Maddie told him before he nodded and kissed her senselessly.

Chapter 30

Christmas Day...

"Where are we going?" Zachary asked from the backseat. It was Christmas Day, the presents had been opened, and the turkey was in the oven.

"To say goodbye to someone I once loved very much," Maddie told him as Nick drove them into the cemetery.

"This is a graveyard," Zachary whispered.

"It's okay, don't be scared. You don't need to whisper," Nick assured him.

"I'm not scared," Zach assured them.

"Good."

Maddie waited until Nick stopped the car and then she pulled her gloves on and gave him an encouraging smile. "I won't be gone long."

"We'll be here," Nick assured her.

"Wait!" Zach called out.

"What is it?" Maddie asked.

"Are you going to say goodbye to your fiancé? The soldier who died?"

Maddie nodded and then asked, "Why?"

Zach looked between them and then shrugged. "Nothing."

Maddie shared a look with Nick and then tried again. "Zach, you can tell us. What's going on in that brain of yours?"

He looked at her and then explained, "I never got to say goodbye."

"To your dad?" she surmised.

Zach nodded, looked forlorn and very sad for a little boy who'd just beat cancer and gained a new family. "I was in the hospital and too sick."

Maddie looked at Nick who added, "Jeff is buried with his wife in Louisiana. Zachary was already here when word came that he was gone."

Maddie thought quickly and then offered, "Zach, would you like to come with me? I know it's not your dad's gravesite, but someone once told me that you can talk to those you love anywhere, the cemetery is just a special place to remember them."

"Could I? Really?"

Maddie looked at Nick who nodded. "Let's all go."

Nick slipped from the car and helped her get Zachary unbuckled and into his warm coat. Nick picked him up and the three of them trudged through the freshly fallen snow until they reached Miah's grave marker.

"There's a bench here," Maddie exclaimed, dusting the snow off and then tearing up as she read the inscription.

Remember Me.

"Who..." she started to question, but the minute she met Nick's eyes, she knew. "You did this?"

"You're learning to let go but there are going to be times when you just need to come here and let your mind settle. Now you don't have to sit on the ground or get into the mud."

Maddie wrapped her arms around him, squeezing Zachary between them. "Thank you."

"Merry Christmas."

Maddie smiled and then kissed him, ignoring the giggles coming from the little boy between them. She kissed him on the forehead, eliciting even more giggles. "Let's try it out."

She sat down and Nick placed Zachary between them. Maddie looked at the grave marker, amazed at how things had changed in such a short amount of time. "Merry Christmas, Miah. I hope you've been watching from up there. It took me a while, but I think I'm finally back in the land of the living."

"Can he hear you?" Zach asked.

Maddie smiled at him and then pulled his stocking cap further down over his ears. "I like to think so. Why don't you try it?"

"Talk to your fiancé?"

"No, silly. Talk to your dad."

"But, he's not here. He won't hear me."

Maddie glanced at Nick and then an idea popped into her head. "I'll take care of that." She turned back to face the grave and started talking again. "Miah, I know you're probably having all sorts of fun up there, but I have a new friend. His name is Zachary and his dad is up there with you. He was a soldier and well, Zachary's been really sick and didn't get a chance to say goodbye. I was wondering if you could take a message to his dad. His name is Jeff from Louisiana."

She turned back to Zach and whispered, "Okay. Just start talking."

Zach looked hesitant for a moment, but then with childlike faith, he started pouring his heart out to his dad, bringing tears to both adults' eyes.

"Dad? It's me Zach. I was really sick so that's why I couldn't say goodbye earlier. I miss you. Lots. I'm with Dr. Nick now and he helped me get all better. I saw grandma yesterday and she's not doing very well. Her memory doesn't work right. Anyway, Aunt Sheila said she would probably be coming up to see you sometime soon so you can watch for her.

"I made a new friend. Her name is Maddie. She and Dr. Nick are going to let me live with them and we're going to be a new family. I don't want you to worry about me. I already love them both and they love me. I'm going to be fine, and I'll make you proud of me. Just like I promised. Bye, daddy."

Zachary ended on a sob and flung himself against Nick's chest. Maddie rubbed his shoulders and murmured words of comfort to him while tears streamed down her face. IT was a cathartic crying from all three, and as their tears finally dried up, there was a new bond between them.

Zachary was exhausted and Nick carried him back to the vehicle silently. They drove all the way home and together, they tucked Zach into bed for a nap before dinner. Once downstairs, Maddie busied herself in the kitchen until Nick came up and wrapped his arms around her from behind.

"Hey, you doing okay?"

Maddie nodded. "Hearing his heart like that...it was really sad, and humbling. He views us as his family now."

"I know."

Maddie put the pan she was holding back on the stove and turned in his arms. "I think it would be the wrong thing to do to upset Zachary's world right now. I'll move in here with you."

"You will?"

Maddie nodded. "I don't know where this thing between us is headed, but I have to be honest with you. The feelings I have for you go way beyond friendship."

Nick hid a smile and asked, "They do? That's good because mine are a tad more complicated than mere friendship, also. In fact, I think I'm falling in love with you."

"Is that even possible this soon?" Maddie asked.

"Why not? Love at first sight and all of that. We've been through a lot in the short time we've known one another. This," Nick moved his finger back and forth between them. "It just feels right."

Maddie nodded in agreement. "Can we still take things slow?"

"As slowly as you need. I'm just glad that we're going to be together and try to make this work. Not just for Zachary. But for us. You deserve to be happy."

"So do you. Merry Christmas, Nick."

"Merry Christmas, Maddie. The first Christmas of many more to come."

Epilogue

Guardian Angel School, January 5th…

Charity entered the schoolroom with a little skip in her step. This was the first time in weeks where she and her other angel friends had been able to get together.

"Joy! Hope! You're here."

"Charity!" The other two angels hugged her, and they all retreated to the chairs in a small circle. "Tell us what's happening with your charge."

Charity beamed at them. She looked around and, when she saw no one else was watching, she pulled out the small graduation pin. "I did it."

"Congratulations! We knew you could," Joy told her.

"Yes. We both passed our tests as well. One more and I'll be able to graduate," Hope added.

"You'll both do fine. So, I want to hear everything. Hope, you go first. How is Claire?"

"Wonderful. She and Travis got married in Las Vegas. I'm sure you can both understand why I didn't drop down to witness the occasion." Hope gave a little shiver of revulsion. "A dirtier place I can't think of."

"I'm in agreement there. But are they happy?" Charity asked.

"Blessedly so. I didn't have to break any rules at all. Humans have an amazing capacity to love."

"I learned the same thing," Charity agreed. "What about you, Joy? Did your little boy get his Christmas wish?"

"Yes, and then some. Not only is Sam's mom happy and in love, but Sam got a dad and a family – his unspoken Christmas wishes. As a benefit, I get to stay with the entire family. Permanently."

"Really?" Charity asked. "Is that even possible?"

"It must be because Matthias made me the same offer. I get to stay with my charges permanently as well."

"Little angel," Matthias said from behind them.

"Matthias. We didn't hear you enter."

"I'm quiet like that. Charity, I'm authorized to make you the same offer as the others. Would you like to stay with Maddie and the others? It will be a lot of work on your part because of the many families that come in and out of their lives."

Charity shook her head, "No, I'm up for the task. I really am. Oh, to stay with Maddie and be there to help others...that is my fondest wish."

"Then I am happy to grant it. You all did a splendid job and learned much along the way. The most important truth was that love is capable of conquering every situation. Love doesn't always mean laughter and rainbows, sometimes there are storms and tragedies, but humans use those dark times to fully appreciate the gift that love is in their lives.

"It is the bond that ties them to their Heavenly Father and only through the acceptance of true love can they begin to comprehend the gift that was given to them thousands of years ago in the birth of our Savior. Choosing to love is an act of free will, but it is the most magical force in the Universe. It is the essence of the Christmas Miracle."

Joy smiled and then joined Sam and his newly acquired family as they exchanged gifts and ate way too much food. It was a normal human celebration, but for Sam and his mother, this year they'd been given a gift that was going to change the course of their lives. Love. The greatest miracle of all.

. . ✑ . .

DID YOU LOVE THIS BOOK? Then you should read the complete set of all 3 books in *Home To You Series* by Morris Fenris. You can read a sample below and grab Book 1, *No Place Like Home*.

. . ✑ . .

CHAPTER 1

Wednesday, December 12th
Central Mountains of Wyoming

Jerricha Ballard, known to her adoring fans as the lead singer for the pop band, *Jericho*, yawned and struggled to see the road sign up ahead. She'd been driving for what felt like two years, but in reality, it had only been for the last two days. She and her traveling partner had spent last night in a small motel, in an even smaller town, paid for in cash. She smiled as she recalled feeling like a criminal on the run as she'd paid for the room and accepted the well-worn key.

She turned the windshield wipers up a notch, trying to clear the rapidly falling snow, but it didn't really seem to help. It was December in Wyoming and she'd been driving in this storm for the last six hours. It was taking a toll on her concentration.

"Does it snow here all winter long?" a voice whined from the passenger seat. "*Brr*. I've never been so cold in my life."

"What did you expect, Cass? Palm trees and sand? This is Wyoming, after all." Jerricha risked a glance at her best friend, Cassidy Peters.

The tires hit a patch of ice and their massive truck slid. Jerricha gripped the steering wheel and corrected its course, peering into the storm.

"Whoa! Take it easy," Cassidy warned her, grabbing the bar above the passenger door. "We've made it this far, don't land us in a ditch now."

Jerricha grimaced, "I've been driving in snow like this since I was sixteen. I can handle it."

"I didn't say you couldn't, but if you wreck Ben's truck, he's going to be doubly ticked off."

Ben Morgan was Jerricha's manager and producer all wrapped into one package. He abhorred traveling on the tour bus and instead chose to drive himself from venue to venue. Jerricha's last three albums had gone platinum, and with the percentage she paid Ben, he'd more than been able to afford the fifty-thousand-dollar truck she'd *borrowed* two nights ago.

"Ben will be fine," Jerricha stated, a note of wishful thinking making its way into her voice. *He's going to be furious with me! Maybe so mad he'll actually make good on his threat to not represent me anymore. That would be such a shame.* She shook her head at the sarcastic thoughts running through her mind and returned her attention to the rapidly deteriorating road conditions.

Cass released a rueful laugh. "That's why he's called over a hundred times in the last two days. Because he knows you're taking such good care of his baby." His baby being the cherry red, double cab, Ford F-350 truck with the lift kit, chrome everything, leather seats, and more amenities than any one person really needs in a vehicle.

"We haven't hurt his precious truck and I even texted him a picture of it at breakfast this morning to prove it."

"Did you tell him where we were?"

"I'm not stupid. Of course not. If I had, he'd have made up some story to get the State Police involved and we would not be almost there now."

Cass looked out the window at the snow-covered landscape and frowned. "Where exactly is it we're going? All I see are mountains and more mountains, and snow. Lots and lots of snow."

"We're headed to Warm Springs, Wyoming," Jerricha replied, relieved when she saw a new road sign up ahead, indicating they were only thirty miles from their destination.

"Warm Springs? What's there?" Cass asked. She'd become best friends with Jerricha several years ago and now went practically everywhere with her. She handled her phone calls, managed the adoring fans always wanting a meet and greet with their favorite pop singer, and, when things got overwhelming, she was the last line of defense between Jerricha and everyone else. Even Ben. Cassidy was the sister Jerricha had never had.

Jerricha nodded, replying softly, "It's where I spent my teenage years. I haven't been here in almost a year. The last time... well, suffice it to say, I could have done without coming back to bury my aunt. Remember last year when I disappeared for two days and everyone was speculating that I'd checked myself into a rehab facility?" When Cassidy nodded, Jerricha grinned. "I came here."

She and Ben had created an elaborate diversion for the press, which had allowed her to travel to Warm Springs for the funeral and fly right back out when it was over. She'd not even been in the town forty-eight hours, something she still regretted. The media had taken the opportunity to speculate, just as she assumed they were doing now. She and Cassidy had made an agreement not to turn on the news or check their social media until they'd reached their destination. Jerricha was taking this time for herself and she wouldn't let anything interfere with her enjoyment of it. She'd missed this place. It was the closest thing she had to a home.

In reality, she'd not been home more often because she refused to subject the town of Warm Springs and her family to the madness her popularity brought. Instead, she and her family kept in touch via video chatting and once in a while she had flown her aunt, uncle, and cousins to a remote vacation destination where photographers and the press were not allowed. But that was before her aunt had suffered a massive stroke that had taken her life a week later. There would be no more family trips. Not for a while. Maybe not ever.

So instead, Jerricha was coming to them this year. The only reason why there wasn't a line of reporters following them now was because she and Cass had skipped out of her Kansas City concert while fans had been screaming for an encore performance.

The band had expected Jerricha to come back onstage, as well, but instead, Cass had snatched Ben's truck keys, packed some of their clothing up during the first half of the concert and tucked their luggage away inside the truck. She'd been waiting for Jerricha at the delivery entrance of the stadium. They were on the highway headed West before anyone had caught on.

They'd stopped at an all-night truck stop on the outskirts of Kansas City and Jerricha had removed the purple streaks from her hair, pulled out the hair extensions, and changed into a pair of well-worn jeans, a flannel shirt over a tank top that she'd had since high school, and a pair of snow boots.

She glanced over at her friend and once again could only shake her head in disbelief. She'd told Cassidy they were heading into the mountains in the middle of the winter, but that evidently hadn't meant much to the city-bred girl from Miami. Cassidy had abandoned her torn leggings, mini skirt and halter top, but her choice of alternate attire wasn't quite what Jerricha had in mind. Cassidy currently wore leather pants, and a bulky sweater with a bright red bra showing through the wide weave pattern. Her hair still sported multi-colored stripes, and her ears and neck were still adorned with lots of jewelry. She would stick out like a sore thumb in Warm Springs. *I'll have to get her some proper clothing as soon as we get there. She's liable to scare half the town dressed this way.*

"So, is all of your family still in Warm Springs?" Cass asked, oblivious to Jerricha's thoughts on her behalf.

Jerricha shook her head. "Not all of them. My parents still live there, and I have an aunt and uncle there in the summer months. They spend the rest of the year in Florida, playing golf."

"Florida. Now that's where we should have gone. Plenty of palm trees, ocean, and tanned guys."

Jerricha chuckled and shook her head. "It's almost Christmas. I haven't been able to spend Christmas in Warm Springs since I was nineteen. That changes this year."

"You must really love this place. But I don't get it. You've never really talked about your childhood. In fact, I don't even know if you have siblings. Why is that?"

Jerricha gave her an incredulous look. "You've fought off the cameras and microphones right alongside me and you can ask that? I don't talk about my hometown because this is mine. I don't want it destroyed by the media and their constant lies."

"I can understand that, but you know it's only a matter of time before someone finds out and comes here looking for you. You can't just disappear without a trace and expect people to let it go."

"I don't have another concert scheduled until after the first of next year. No one will be looking for me. And I hardly look like the lead singer from *Jericho*. Even if they come looking, they won't be looking for a mountain girl with normal hair, no tattoos, and no makeup on." *I hope. Maybe I should call Ben and make sure he's running interference for me.*

"You're thinking of calling Ben," Cass said, watching her carefully.

Jerricha nodded. "I probably need to, but..."

"But..."

"He does know where I'm from and if he thinks this is where I've gone, he won't hesitate to come here and that would be a disaster. I'll call him when we get there."

"What are you going to say?" Cassidy asked with wide eyes.

Jerricha shrugged. "I have no idea. Maybe I'll just tell him I quit." At the look of horror on Cassidy's face, Jerricha sighed and then told her, "I'll figure something out. Don't worry. As for siblings, I have two brothers. Kaedon is four years older than me and runs a construction company that specializes in restoring old homes and such. He travels quite a bit, but he still has a home in Warm Springs. Rylor is a social worker in Cheyenne."

"Wow. Two brothers. I never knew that. Like I said, you rarely talk about your family."

Jerricha smiled, deciding to keep the fact that Rylor was also her twin a secret for now. Instead, she replied, "I've gotten so used to keeping my personal life a secret, not even the band members know about my personal life."

"Afraid they'll talk to the wrong person?"

Jerricha nodded. "You know it. The band was put together by the record label when I was nineteen. We seemed to all work together really well in the early days and before we knew it, the band was a success."

"Yeah, but don't you think your fans will get tired of you all refusing to give interviews and do the award shows?"

"Maybe, but given that our last record went platinum in the first week, I'm not really buying into the panic that Ben likes to peddle. A little mystery surrounding myself and the band members keeps people interested."

"Yeah, well, one of these days your little secret is going to get out. What then?"

"I'll cross that bridge when I come to it. Besides, who knows how much longer the band will be together? In case you haven't noticed, some of the band members don't exactly exude high morals."

Cassidy grimaced. "I've noticed. So has the rest of the world."

"Yeah, I'm getting tired of hearing Ben yell about legal fees and such. I wish they'd all just settle down and stop acting out."

"Maybe this is just a phase they're going through," Cassidy offered.

"Maybe." Jerricha turned her attention back to the road. The snowdrifts on the road's sides were a testament to how much snow had fallen in recent days. It was still coming down strong and she was anxious to get to town and off the roads before the storm got any worse. She was anxious to see her parents and start relaxing. It had been way too many months since she'd even thought about doing nothing and the idea was really appealing. *Almost home. Just a few more miles.*

Chapter 2

"So...," Cassidy drew the word out and then changed the subject. "Don't the townsfolk know who you are and why haven't they told anyone?"

Jerricha smiled at Cass. "You've never met the people of Warm Springs. They protect their own and they hate reporters. Years ago, a man from Warm Springs, Godfrey Merkel, decided he could do a better job as governor than the current man sitting in Cheyenne and he ran for office. The reporters descended on the town with their news trucks and lights... It quickly turned into a circus."

"I can see why that might have been annoying to the townsfolk, but hate? That seems a little strong."

"It's not. The reporters were so intent on digging up dirt on the man, nothing was off limits. They completely took over the town. They parked their trucks wherever, were constantly asking everyone questions, and left a trail of destruction behind them. The final straw was when one of the news trucks' drivers, arriving late at night, thought he'd found a nice vacant patch of grass to park his truck on for the night."

"What he'd do, wind up in the city park?" Cass asked.

Jerricha shook her head. "Much worse. He was parked in the cemetery, right on top of the would-be governor's late wife's grave. The press had been in town for a week, and everyone was sick and tired of the hoopla they created. Desecrating the cemetery was the final straw.

"The sheriff, along with half a dozen men from town, had had enough and ran every last media person and photographer out of town."

"Didn't they just come right back?" Cass had witnessed firsthand how tenacious the press could be.

"They tried, but there's only one road into and out of Warm Springs. The sheriff and men from town set up a blockade and then took control of it, armed with rifles. He even deputized them to make it all legal and such. After a few days, everyone gave up and they never came back."

"What happened to the man who wanted to be governor?"

"Godfrey? Well, he decided that level of politics wasn't for him and when the position of mayor became available, he ran and won. He's been mayor ever since."

"But how does that keep you protected?" Cassidy wanted to know.

"It just does. Not everyone knows who I am and those that do... they guard my secret very closely. You said it yourself. No one would recognize me if I'm dressed like this."

"But the minute you open your mouth and sing anything, everyone will know exactly who you are," Cassidy argued.

Jerricha's throaty, raspy voice was her trademark sound and easily recognizable by anyone who listened to popular music. "I'll just have to keep my singing relegated to the showers then, won't I?"

Cassidy chuckled and shook her head. "I'll believe that when I see it." Jerricha's life was one big song. She ate, slept, and breathed music of one sort or another. "I bet I catch you singing in the first twenty-hours we're here."

"Maybe, but I'm certain my secret is safe here. You'll understand that once you meet some of the townsfolk. Nicer people don't exist on the planet."

Jerricha put on her blinker and slowly navigated the turn onto the road leading to her hometown. The place where she could be herself. Her sanctuary. The one place in the world where she could count on being accepted for who she was as a person, not as a celebrity.

"Cass, I hate to ask this, but it's kind of necessary. We need to turn our cell phones completely off. You can turn it back on whenever you need to make a call, but I wouldn't put it past Ben to try and track our phones and I just want to be alone for a while."

"Hey, you don't have to justify things to me. Truthfully, I don't know how you put up with the constant attention and having your privacy invaded all of the time. It's no wonder you're close to a breakdown."

Jerricha sighed in agreement. Five nights ago, she'd collapsed while taking a break halfway through her St. Louis show and she'd barely been able to go back out on stage and finish, albeit, sitting on a hastily procured stool. She'd been on tour for the last ten months, and in between concerts and traveling around the world, she'd also found time to record a new album of Christmas songs that would be released on December twenty-first. Nine days from now.

Ben had wanted to add a whirlwind promotional Christmas tour to her already full schedule, but she'd put her foot down and refused. Kansas City had been her last scheduled performance on this tour, and she'd already announced she would take a sabbatical for the entire next year.

Ben had been furious with that decision, sure that she would become a has-been if she didn't keep producing new songs for her adoring and fickle fans. Jerricha didn't agree and she was willing to take that risk. She was tired, mentally, emotionally, and physically. Taking a year off had been her choice and since she could very well afford to do so, she wasn't seeking anyone's advice. She just wanted to be left alone and have time to find herself once again.

As for the band, well, they were all fine with having some time to party wherever the wind took them, and she knew that several of them were headed across the pond to hang out around Europe for a while. Part of her hoped they would all find other things to do during the next twelve months. If that happened, Ben would have no choice but to give her a shot at a solo career.

As far as the media was concerned, she was supposed to be flying to Tahiti to meet up with Bryce Lansing, a solo male pop singer who had shown an interest in her at a celebrity fundraiser she'd attended six months earlier. Since he was represented by the same record label, they'd been thrown together and rumors had been leaked that she and Bryce were having a secret relationship and would be making it public right after the first of the year.

The record label had been trying to boost Bryce's popularity and connecting him to Jerricha had been just the thing. His latest album had risen sharply in the polls, reaching the Top 10 within just a few weeks of his name being tied to hers. It hadn't really done a thing for Jerricha's career. Her fan base was one she'd been building since she'd first broken onto the music scene at nineteen.

The record label wanted to continue the façade, even hinting that they'd love to see a fake engagement sometime during January. Jerricha was adamantly against that idea, but Ben hadn't listened to her protests. She'd decided to take matters into her own hands.

She'd advanced her holiday plans a few weeks, and she wouldn't apologize for that to anyone. Warm Springs was her refuge and she was going to hibernate here for the winter, reconnect with her family and friends, and hopefully find the motivation to pick her life back up once again when the year was up. In a week or so, she'd send a message to one of the social media sites that usually made her life so miserable. She'd tell them of her terrible breakup with Bryce and then disappear for the next year. By the time she reappeared, her supposed breakup with Bryce would be old news and she could get back to her normal life.

Or not. She'd had fame and fortune and it wasn't all it was purported to be. She could easily go the rest of her life without signing another autograph or smiling for the camera alongside another celebrity looking to boost their popularity by being seen with her. In short, she was tired of being used.

As the small town came into view half an hour later, Jerricha felt a peace settle over her soul she'd not been able to find anywhere else in the world. "Welcome to Warm Springs."

She slowed the truck at the top of the small hill, bringing the vehicle to a stop on the snow-covered road, so that she could take in the familiar sight of mountains surrounding the small community. Snow covered the rooftops and lights already burned brightly in most of the homes, even though there were still several hours before the sun would disappear behind the mountains. Smoke rose in wisps from fireplaces and Jerricha couldn't stop the feeling of peace that settled over her soul. *Home. This is home.*

"It's like something out of a magazine," Cass whispered, the sight before them awe-inspiring to a city girl like her.

Jerricha nodded and then told her, "This place is sacred to me. No one knows about it except Ben and now you."

"The band members haven't been here before?"

Jerricha frowned and shook her head sharply. "No. I can't stand to be around those guys when we're not on stage. There was a time when we could laugh and joke with one another, but lately, they seem to be more into drugs and alcohol and women. I don't want any part of that lifestyle. Besides, can you imagine them in a place like this? No adoring groupies clamoring for their autograph or a quick tour of the bus. No photographers shoving cameras in their faces anytime they went out in public. They would be bored out of their minds within an hour, and they'd never appreciate the town for the gem it is."

"I've noticed there seems to be more and more partying happening. Is that why you stopped spending the night on the tour bus and started getting hotel rooms?"

Jerricha nodded. "Exactly. I explained it all to Ben and told him about my concerns. He assured me it's just a phase the guys are going through. Once they get used to how popular we are, they'll settle down and things will be back to normal."

"You don't believe him," Cass stated.

"No, I don't. I think Ben's assuming the guys will wake up one morning and realize how they're screwing up their lives, but they won't. They enjoy all the negative attention. I'm the one who's holding them back from even greater fame and fortune because I'm being the goody two shoes. They're afraid I'm going to try to go out on my own. My contract is up at the end of December and I haven't signed the renewal yet. I'm not sure I want to. I've kind of thought about going out on my own and doing my own thing for a while. No more tours. I can write and record..."

"That's not the worst idea I've ever heard. I mean, you write most of the songs now and sing them. You could become a solo act rather easy."

"Ben says the record label doesn't want a solo act. He doesn't, either. He wants to fill the stage with lights and videos, guitar licks, drum solos... the entire band experience."

Cass shook her head and made a sound of disapproval. "What do you want? I mean, without your voice, there is no *Jericho*. So, from where I sit, you hold all the cards."

Jerricha started up the truck again and headed down into the town. She couldn't stop thinking about Cass's question. *What do I want? What will make me truly happy?*

She'd kept herself from going down that mind path in the past, but now she had a little over two weeks in which to explore her feelings. Two weeks to take stock of her dreams and aspirations and measure them against the life she was currently living. Two weeks to measure them against the life she wanted to live. Two weeks to find the answer to Cass's question and set a course for her future happiness.

Chapter 3
Warm Springs, Wyoming

"See you, Mr. James," a group of teenagers called to him as they rushed out of the school building, grabbing handfuls of freshly fallen snow and throwing it at one another.

"Bye, kids. Drive safe."

"Always do, Mr. James. See you Monday."

"Bye, Coach."

Logan waved and stepped back inside the building, shaking the snow from his hair as he headed for the school offices. He walked to the large windows behind his desk and watched as the last of the students left the parking lot. *Drive safe kids. I don't want to hear of any accidents because of this snow.*

"Do you care if I head on home now?" Stella Ziegs asked.

Logan James turned and smiled at the school secretary. "Not at all." Stella was a well-known icon at the local high school, having been there since before Logan had been a student there a dozen years earlier. Her hair was grayer and her step a little slower these days, but without her organizational prowess, Logan knew his job would be much harder.

"The last bus left a few minutes ago and based on the vehicles still in the parking lot, I think most of the teachers have left, as well. Go home and enjoy a good book." Stella always complained how she didn't have time to read for the fun of it. Well, Mother Nature had just provided her an extra day and a half to do just that. A roaring fire. A good book. Hot Chocolate. Logan could even see himself spending the rest of the day in such a fashion.

It was barely one o'clock in the afternoon, but the winter storm that had been forecasted to arrive the next day had arrived early. The school day had already been in session when the first flakes started to fall, and within the first hour, over four inches of new snow had blanketed the valley with no signs of slowing down or stopping in the near future. It had fallen to Logan as the principal to notify everyone that the school day would be cut short. As he'd walked around to the various classes, he could only smile at the students' responses. Cheering. Slapping of hands above their heads. Teachers closing textbooks and announcing there would be no homework for this first major storm of the year. More cheers and smiles.

As students and teachers filed out of the building, there had been an air of excitement that had become infectious. There was only one more week of school before Christmas break would begin, and this unexpected vacation time had everyone, young and old alike, looking forward to building snowmen, skiing, and the Christmas holiday.

Logan had stationed himself at the exit doors, cautioning young drivers to go slowly and arrive home safely. He had only been back in Warm Springs since the beginning of the school year, but he took his responsibilities to the students very serious. It was his intention to make sure all the students got safely home before the temperatures dropped and the snow-covered roads became impassable.

Stella slipped her coat on with a smile. "I love snow days."

Logan nodded. "Me too. Get out of here and I'll see you Monday, weather permitting."

Snow days were one of the benefits of coaching and working for the Fremont County School District. Warm Springs was located in the mountains, nestled in a small valley with only one road leading into and out of the town. To the east of the small town was a popular ski resort that brought many tourists and sports enthusiasts to the area. While the town only boasted a population of around fifteen hundred people, the surrounding mountain communities brought the student population of his secondary school to well over five hundred. Warm Springs held the secondary school, with a dual campus consisting of a middle school and a high school. The elementary school was located about ten miles outside of the town, halfway between Warm Springs and the next closest mountain town of Drummond. The two campuses also served the surrounding communities, some close to thirty miles away. A bus system transported the students to and from the neighboring towns, with some students riding nearly an hour each way, making it even more critical that the school day ended with plenty of time for everyone to arrive home while there was still some daylight left.

"Mr. James, are you heading out soon?" Bill, the janitor, called to him from the end of the hallway.

"Just as soon as I clear some papers off my desk. How about you?"

Bill nodded and leaned on the broom he held in his hands. "I told the wife I'd be home before it got dark and started to freeze. She worries about my driving these days."

Logan smiled easily. He'd known Bill and Tammy for as long as he could remember, and he wasn't sure of his exact age, but he knew Bill was at least seventy, maybe even a few years older. According to the information Logan received when he moved back to Warm Springs and took over the job of running the secondary school, the previous principal had tried to get Bill to retire, but he'd adamantly refused. He enjoyed being around the kids and taking care of the school had been his job for his entire adult life. He had no intention of stopping until he simply couldn't do the job any longer.

Logan waved at the man and headed back to his office. Clearing off his desk didn't take all that long, and within an hour, he shoved his arms into his winter jacket and headed for the parking lot. He climbed into his truck after dusting off the accumulated snow on the windows and headed for the only grocery store in town.

Since moving back to Warm Springs, he'd taken up residence in his childhood home, left vacant when his parents had retired to Arizona, where the weather was much warmer and kinder to his mother's arthritis. He'd traveled to Arizona for the Thanksgiving holiday, and they would be coming to Wyoming for Christmas. That gave him just over a week to unpack the rest of his boxes and put the house back into some sort of order.

Life had been hectic since his arrival in Warm Springs, with the beginning of the school year, and the sudden vacancy of a football coach. The Warm Springs Wildcats football team had taken second in the state the year before and had been projected as a serious contender for the state title this school year. But their longtime coach had been diagnosed with Stage 3 Leukemia during summer break and was currently seeking treatment somewhere in California.

Logan had not only been the captain of the football team and quarterback in high school, but he'd played college ball, and, at one point in time, he'd been a second-string quarterback on a professional team. That was until he'd torn his rotator cuff. Surgery had repaired the torn ligaments, but the team doctors had refused to clear him to return to the field for fear another injury would be irreparable. His football career had been finished. During his months of rehabilitation, he'd gone back to school and started his Master's program, taking his parents' advice and turning his love for kids and sports into a career. Teaching.

The fact that he'd coached the team to the State Championship just last weekend didn't matter as much as seeing the excitement on the kids' faces when they had been awarded the trophy. The entire town was still celebrating their victory. Logan refused to take any credit for their winning streak, believing that their past training had been far more instrumental than his one season of guidance. Several of the boys were being considered for college scholarships and he only prayed they would have better luck in pursuing their dreams than he'd had.

He parked in the lot, admiring a bright red oversized truck as he did so. The vehicle wasn't from Warm Springs and he briefly wondered whose relatives were visiting this early before the holidays. It was a little too soon for tourists to start descending upon the town. They usually didn't arrive until the week before Christmas and would then stay until after ringing in the New Year.

The doors of the store were decorated with festive bows, garland, and multi-colored lights. A large Christmas tree sat just to the inside of them, reminding Logan that he still needed to get his own tree up and decorated. Hopefully before his parents arrived, or he'd never hear the end of it. His mother was a hopeless romantic and Christmas was her favorite time of year. As such, it was also one of his favorite holidays. *I've just been so busy with the State Championship and school board meetings... Well, Mother Nature has seen fit to give me a nice five-day holiday and I should take advantage of it.*

He made a mental note to head out the next day and locate the perfect tree. He could go find one up in the mountains, but Warm Springs boasted an easier solution. On the outskirts of town, the Millers had a tree farm, and whilst most of their Christmas trees were shipped out of state each year, they always kept plenty of trees for the locals who wanted to cut down their own. That was where his parents had always obtained their tree, and he would do the same this year. *I'll just be doing it alone. I'm getting kind of tired of doing things all alone. I'm thirty. I should be married and have a couple of kids by now.*

But circumstances hadn't worked out that way, and even though Logan had come close, even being engaged for all of three weeks' time, he was still very single. And looking. *Might have thought about that before moving to a town where everyone is already spoken for or can't wait to get out of town.*

The town of Warm Springs didn't actually have any single, unattached females of marrying age at the moment. There were several unmarried people still living in the town, but most of them worked in other places and only used Warm Springs as a stopping place between jobs. They weren't ready to settle down and start a family. Logan didn't consider himself and them in the same category at all. *Maybe I should add a bride to my Christmas list. Maybe there really is a Santa Claus.*

Three Christmas Angels Series

Christmas Angel Joy
Christmas Angel Hope
Christmas Angel Charity

. . ⚜ . .

IF YOU ENJOY MY BOOK(s), kindly help me by posting and sharing review(s) about my work – thank you!

Thank You

Dear Reader,

Thank you for choosing to read my books out of the thousands that merit reading. I recognize that reading takes time and quietness, so I am grateful that you have designed your lives to allow for this enriching endeavor, whatever the book's title and subject.

Now more than ever before, reader reviews and social media play vital roles in helping individuals make their reading choices. If any of my books have moved you, inspired you, or educated you, please share your reactions with others by posting a review as well as via email, Facebook, Twitter, Goodreads,—or even old-fashioned face-to-face conversation! And when you receive my announcement of my new book, please pass it along. Thank you.

For updates about New Releases, as well as exclusive promotions, visit my website and sign up for the VIP mailing list: www.morrisfenrisbooks.com[1]

I invite you to visit my Facebook page often facebook.com/AuthorMorrisFenris[2] where I post not only my news, but announcements of other authors' work.

For my portfolio of books on your favorite platform, please search for and visit my Author Page by typing Morris Fenris in the search bar of the relevant website.

You can also contact me by email: authormorrisfenris@gmail.com

With profound gratitude, and with hope for your continued reading pleasure,

Morris Fenris
Self-Published Author

---

1.   http://www.morrisfenrisbooks.com

2.   https://www.facebook.com/AuthorMorrisFenris/

Did you love *Christmas Angel Charity*? Then you should read *Sara in Montana*[3] by Morris Fenris!

What happens when a California girl in the middle of a crisis meets a Montana guy?

Sara wished for a husband for Christmas this year and then married her boss. Now she is running for her life from him, with a warrant out for her arrest, and really needs a miracle to save her. To top off her week, she finds herself in the middle of a Montana snowstorm and sicker than she's ever been.

Trent quit the FBI to return home and became a sheriff. As the most eligible bachelor in Castle Peaks, he's had his share of women chase him but has been disinterested; until now. He has a sworn duty to protect the town's citizens and assist other agencies in doing the same. When faced with a suspect in a criminal case, will he make the arrest or lead with his heart?

---

3. https://books2read.com/u/mYGzgw

4. https://books2read.com/u/mYGzgw

Join Sara Brownell as she runs for her life, straight into the waiting arms of local sheriff Trent Harding. Throw in a life-size nativity and plenty of snow, and watch the magic of Christmas come to life.

See how Sara forever changes the lives of Trent, as well as those around him.

Read more at https://www.facebook.com/AuthorMorrisFenris/.

Morris Fenris
Author

About the Author

With a lifelong love of reading and writing, Morris Fenris loves to let his imagination paint pictures in a wide variety of genres. His current book list includes everything from Christian romance, to an action-packed Western romance series, to inspirational and Christmas holiday romance.

His novels are filled with emotion, and while there is both heartbreak and humor, the stories are always uplifting.

Read more at https://www.facebook.com/AuthorMorrisFenris/.